Love and Other Disappointments

Some of these stories have been previously published in a different form including:

"PLENTY OF FISH." Short Story, *The New Quarterly*. 2020.
"ZUG-ZWANG." Short Story, *Antigonish Review*. 2019.
"HARD TO SWALLOW." Short Story, *Prairie Fire*. 2015.
"SHELTER." Short Story, *The Newfoundland Quarterly*. 2014.
"ALL THINGS IN COMMON." Short Story, *Paragon*. 2014.
"INSIDE PASSAGES." Short Story, *The Lamp*. 2014.
"BODILY FUNCTIONS." Short Story, *The Nashwaak Review*. 2013.

Love and Other Disappointments

Stories

Heather Paul

Library and Archives Canada Cataloguing in Publication

Title: Love and other disappointments : stories / Heather Paul.

Names: Paul, Heather (Novelist), author.

Identifiers: Canadiana (print) 20230577784 | Canadiana (ebook) 20230577792 |
ISBN 9781989689622 (softcover) | ISBN 9781989689660 (EPUB)

Subjects: LCGFT: Short stories.

Classification: LCC PS8631.A84969 L68 2024 | DDC C813/.6—dc23

Printed and bound in Canada on 100% recycled paper.

Now Or Never Publishing
901, 163 Street
Surrey, British Columbia
Canada V4A 9T8

nonpublishing.com
Fighting Words.

We gratefully acknowledge the support of the Canada Council for the Arts
and the British Columbia Arts Council for our publishing program.

For Aurora, Blaise, and Jasper

Between these covers everything is real; nothing is true.
Or everything is true; nothing is real. Or something like that.

Table of Contents

PLENTY
OF
FISH

PLENTY OF FISH

I saw the best minds of my generation… Lindsey thinks of the opening line of Ginsberg's "Howl." It keeps weaseling into her head like the chorus of a pop song or a mantra. What was the rest of it? *…starving, hysterical…* She turns in the passenger seat to ask Scott if he knows the next line. He holds up two fingers, barks instructions into his phone.

She looks out the window, sees mostly harried drivers drinking out of paper cups, takes in the ribbons of asphalt stacked four lanes deep, the absence of trees.

"I gotta get a new bulb for my aquarium lamp," Scott whispers, holding the phone away from his face and pulling into Walmart in Etobicoke. His jaw tightens. He pulls the phone away from his face and shakes his head as though it were the one responsible for the dominoing incompetence.

It's nearly six, but late July, so still plenty of light. The parking lot holds the heat of the day and it rises up through Lindsey's pink flip-flops, through the soles of her feet. She tries not to think of the million other things she could be doing right now. She's running errands with Scott on her day off, unwittingly eavesdropping on his fractured conversations and feeling as superfluous as male nipples. Maybe she's just hungry. Since having a child she's grown accustomed to regular mealtimes. She's come all the way to Toronto for dinner and to spend the night with Scott, a friend of a friend she's met up with a few times in the last month. A kind of spill-over third date from a connection courtesy of her pal, Marie, who eventually married the guy they knew from the commerce program who is friends with Scott.

The three of them had dropped in on Lindsey unexpectedly one night at the end of June when the branches of the mulberry tree in the backyard of her rental house hung heavy with fruit.

Swollen berries dangled from overhanging branches, plummeted intermittently onto the table and the patio. Left purple-red splotches that looked like sores. Lindsey apologized. Felt the need to explain, to excuse her neglect. But didn't bother. The "child-free" could never understand that sometimes it was difficult just to keep the kitchen table clean. She swabbed a damp cloth over the surface, collecting spent berries into an old ice-cream tub for the compost. Marie pushed her chair back from the table to protect her white jeans and squished further, with the heel of her denim-striped espadrilles, those that had already dive-bombed the paving stones. Lindsey shook a branch, gathering handfuls of berries into a wire colander that once belonged to her grandmother. Took them into the kitchen where, in bare feet and cut-offs, her one-year-old son on her hip, she'd thrown together a sweet-tart crisp. Marie leaned up against the sink as she rinsed the heels of her shoes and whispered to Lindsey, *He's been lonely since the divorce we thought maybe…*

Scott raved about the crisp. He'd played with Sam too. Had put his napkin over his face for peek-a-boo. In yellow, mulberry-stained Crocs, Sam's chubby legs stomped through the juicy patio minefield, Marie recoiling with each squish. Later in the evening, amid mosquito slapping and Sam's squeals and giggles, Scott had pulled him around the yard in the wooden wagon that had been Lindsey's thirty years earlier. They drank cold Coronas, limes wedged down the throats of the bottles. Feet up on empty, overturned flowerpots. It had almost felt like something.

Her parents were the sort to hold onto things like that wagon, like her camp trunk, her grandmother's dishes. The past was so much clutter. No one coveted their Nana's bone china teacups. Sure, people still wanted things, the same things probably, so long as they seemed different than whatever came before. Out of wedlock baby shaming had gone the way of girdles and polished silver. Lindsey was constantly refusing cardboard boxes of newspaper wrapped glasses, teacups. Fish forks and floral lidded tureens. Linens. *Well, take it. Save it for when you are settled*, her mother would euphemistically encourage, patting her shoulder. As if a proper marriage with a china pattern registry was something to which Lindsey aspired.

Anyway, Scott was attractive. Charming. Available.

Lindsey had begged her parents to babysit Sam for Friday overnight. Pumped and pumped her teats of milk until they hurt and hung like deflated balloons against her chest. Had packed suitcases for the both of them, farmed the dog out to a friend, written pages of instructions for her parents to follow. Handed them a cooler of bottled breast milk, and finally, drank a third coffee and drove the two hours from north of the city to meet Scott for noon. She felt like she'd already lived a full day before arriving. What a girl had to do these days to get laid.

Ever since she got to Toronto it's been one thing after another. First, he had to finish emailing, then he had to check his phone messages, then he had to pick up BMW parts at the garage, then his dry cleaning, and now a new lamp for his fish. He had told her he was taking the day off, that this Friday he'd be free. Like he couldn't have done some of this crap before she arrived or after she left? He is busy. She is busy. We are all busy. So damn busy being busy. Scott, everyone she knows really, seems like a bullet speeding somewhere full of direction, with purpose, but without target. *Madness,* that's what the next line is. That came before *starving hysterical—destroyed by madness.*

Sorry, Scott mouths, holding his phone-free hand out for hers and directing her toward the pet supplies aisle. She tags along after him, watching him read the back of aquarium light boxes. Watching the hoards of people, the salad bowl of mixed ethnicities wandering through shelves stacked high as though they were following the righteous path of consumerism through a space-age labyrinth, seeking salvation with useless junk.

Yet, all the headscarves and black hair delights Lindsey. What a relief to have escaped from the land of beige. She will fill herself with new sights, some conversation, dinner downtown, sex. It would totally be worth her while. Eventually.

"Who are you talking to?"

"Deloitte, work." He makes his lamp selection and they wind their way through the aisles to the express checkout. From where they are standing at one end, to the window of the golden arches at the other end of the big box store, is probably the length of a football field.

Lindsey wishes she'd parked at a friend's house and met him downtown. While she had intended to stay at his house, the one overlooking the ravine he loved to brag about, the one he used to share with his wife before she got cervical cancer and then recovered and then divorced, Lindsey didn't think she was going to be dragged around doing chores all afternoon. She'd hoped to maximize her free time away from Sam, do some things for herself. Spend a couple of hours at the art gallery, read a magazine and enjoy a decent latte. She reminds herself that romance will never be convenient for a woman with a child. Besides, she likes the way Scott's face contours in from his cheekbones, the way the stubble persists in the cleft of his chin. The way his eyes dart back and forth as he paces like an emergency room doctor during his intense phone conversations about what, she couldn't imagine, but was pretty sure wasn't life or death.

She stands behind him in the interminable line up. He scrutinizes the sundries hanging on wire prongs flanking the exit funnel and apologizes to Lindsey for having to make another call. Asks to speak to Priscilla on the fourteenth floor. Walmartians stare at him; they too can't help eavesdropping. Lindsey picks up a package of gum. Thinks, *I saw the best minds of my generation, destroyed by madness, starving hysterical…naked!* Yes, *naked.* She smiles.

Scott looks at the green package in her hand, lifts his chin away from the mouthpiece, says, "I only have enough cash for the bulb." He should have stopped at the bank he says. He only ever uses cash—it's the only way to properly keep track.

Lindsey reaches for her wallet, waves her debit card, takes the lamp and says, Don't worry about it. Scott mouths thank you through a grin, plugs his one ear and backs away from the cash register. There's something about the warmth in his brown eyes, the way they look at her, open and expectant. Like they could wrap around and hold her. Reassure her that she wouldn't always have to work so hard.

Back at the house, Scott replaces the aquarium light and turns it on, illuminating the one remaining fish. Not counting the algae eater that moves along the inside of the tank with its creamy open mouth suctioned to the glass.

Lindsey stands in front of the aquarium watching the silver fish with the translucent tail as it swims back and forth between glass walls. The bored little thing, its whole life laid out before him. This fish inside this tank. This tank inside this house. This house inside this city.

Scott slips his hand up her blouse at the small of her back. Lindsey points to an acoustic guitar leaning up against a mostly empty bookshelf. Light brown, mother of pearl inlay circling the sound hole. "You play?"

"Just learning. Here I'll play you something."

Guitar perched on his knee, Scott plays a very clunky "Smoke on the Water." Lindsey laughs.

"I'm just shittin' ya." He plays a second song. She recognizes *After the Goldrush*, Neil Young. His voice is soft and clear. Gentle. And, from what Lindsey can tell, perfectly on key.

"You're really good."

"Jeez. Don't act so surprised. I used to sing in the choir at my mom's church. Not recently. When I was a kid."

Scott tells Lindsey he needs a shower. Squeezes her and kisses her mouth. She pulls away. He grabs her hands and tries to draw her toward the bathroom. Removes his clothes. Makes sexy eyes at her.

"C'mon. Let me soap you up."

"I'm really hungry. Where should we go tonight?"

"This is just an appetizer, we can also have dessert," he says, raising eyebrows in mock suggestiveness.

Lindsey won't take the bait. If she gets in that shower there goes dinner. She at least wants to be fed before being fucked. She wishes he'd put his clothes back on. Wishes he wasn't so eager to get down to it. She isn't some desperate baby mama.

She retreats to the kitchen hoping for a drink. A glass of wine would be nice. She's brought a bottle of wine as a gift. Wouldn't exactly be polite to go opening and swilling it now. Though, that is exactly what she wants to do. She looks through cupboards. They expose yellow and black labels on peanut butter, pasta, soup. Even *No Name* ketchup and mustard in the fridge. A bottle of vodka sits behind glass doors in the butler's pantry. Lindsey can think of nothing to explain the tins of *No Name* in an investment banker's kitchen other than an inner stinginess. She pours a couple shots over some ice in a heavy crystal glass that clinks on the granite when she sets it down. Then, she guzzles her vodka, thinks better of it and brushes her teeth at the steel sink with the grand looping faucet.

Scott comes up behind her at the counter wearing only his towel and a humid cloud of Irish Spring. Cups her breasts large and swollen now with unexpressed milk and plucks at her nipples. So, they'd have sex and then they'd go out. Climax is swift for both, their actual coupling brief, and when Lindsay comes, milk squirts from her over-ripe breasts. She apologizes, is embarrassed by such intimacy in front of someone she doesn't even really know. Scott says he wondered what the wet was then takes her in his mouth and sucks, which both surprises and horrifies her, though she allows it. It feels somehow like an offering. She collects and reassembles her clothes strewn around the kitchen while Scott dresses in his bedroom. He calls to her from down the hall.

"I know today probably wasn't the most exciting day of your life, but I need you to know that I'm a busy guy. I'm thirty-four, too old to pretend to be something I'm not. Time is money and I like to make the most of both."

She says, don't worry, it's fine, watches him from the doorway as he flops back on the bed, his towel again wrapping his lower torso, his abdominal muscles defined in creases. Money is a necessary evil, she supposes. Busyness too. And, she supposes also, that she wouldn't mind more of it. Day care costs are killing her.

"Hey Lindsey," he calls out. "I'm tired. It's been a hell of a week. Sure you don't want to stay in, watch some TV? I could make us some pasta?"

Lindsey's stomach bristles and shrinks like she's swallowed a puffer fish. She thinks of the black and yellow boxes of macaroni in his cupboards. "I understand you're tired. I know you're very busy, but I've arranged babysitting and come all this way and it feels like we haven't really even done anything or spent any time together." Oh no. Now she is whining. Or is she? Is this what it means to assert oneself? She walks over to the fish tank, bends down and examines the contents once again. In the tan gravel an aquanaut bubbles up and down in the back right corner by the filter.

"We spent the whole afternoon together!"

"You're right." It was a large tank for one fish and that weird sucking creature that looked like a tadpole hybrid with spots. "Here's the thing. I don't get out very often and I'd really like to go somewhere besides East Side Mario's to eat. Nothing fancy, just out."

"Okay, okay. I know a great little place in Kensington, tasty inexpensive food."

"Do you think you'll ever get more fish?"

Scott says he isn't sure.

By this time, it's dark outside, still hot, but evening traffic as they drive east from Etobicoke is more relaxed. He takes her hand and kisses it. She rubs the joint of his thumb with hers. As they stroll together past the many bustling restaurants of Kensington market, smells of burritos and frying pakoras, the remnants of the day's fish market mingle in the heady air above the sidewalks and "Howl," like an earworm, filters through her mind. She rearranges the words, plays around with the opening line in her head.

A joyless waiter in a long, white half-apron escorts them to the patio. Scott reaches under the table and squeezes her knee.

Tires squeal in the near distance. A horn honks. Reggae pumps from an upstairs apartment.

"This is nice. It's nice not to be rushing around doing something important."

"Yeah," Lindsey says, "sometimes people get so busy doing they forget about being."

"I never thought of it that way. Cool, Lindsey."

A dreadlocked, tattooed couple walks past them. A puff of weed and cigarette smoke wafts over their table. They sit in the dark on the outdoor patio smiling politely at each other over a flickering tea light, eating pumpkin ravioli dyed black with squid ink and drinking a bottle of "good value wine." Lindsey begins to feel more comfortable, settles into herself and shares her poetic revision.

"I saw the best minds of my generation destroyed by money, besuited, creeping through the bald, ethereal streets at dawn looking for the entrance to Deloitte."

"Huh?" Scott's phone rings. He checks the caller ID and lets it go to voice mail. Stuffs a big ravioli into his mouth. Wipes his face with a cloth napkin and spreads it back over his lap. Lindsey imagines having to pretreat with laundry detergent the black and orange lip streaks across the white square.

"'Howl,' you know, Allen Ginsberg? I was talking about it earlier today."

"Some friend of yours?"

"Yeah," Lindsey says, crossing two fingers, "we're like this."

She looks at her quarter-full glass of cabernet sauvignon, examines the label of the empty bottle. It will be hours until she's sober enough to drive and here she is, miles away from home with her breasts so very full.

SHELTER

Shelter

All April long we played board games and made arts and crafts, watching, and waiting through back-room windows for the lawn to absorb the melting snow. The yard was no good for play when wet; not that it mattered anyway since we'd been on lock-down for nearly three weeks. We could only look outside, could only imagine what forms might spring up, what it might feel like to spin madly around with our arms outstretched in the cool breeze of morning, what possibilities might wait for us on the other side of those panes of glass.

By May the woman we'd been locked down to protect went back to her husband so the boys and I, it was all boys that summer, roped off a garden plot in the corner of the yard. We did the best we could to turn the soil over with a pitchfork and a few dented snow shovels and the rest of the mostly useless garden tool donations. We fought with rocks and roots, toiled and tilled till the dirt grew soft and crumbled, its earthy smell a prelude to the peat and sheep's manure. And though the air was still pretty cool, the boys shed first their jackets and then their hoodies, and the sun and the digging kept them warm.

The back of the package gave instructions which I read aloud and translated into simple measurements that would make the same sense to the five-year-old as to the fifteen-year-old: keep soil loose, make rows, push seeds down one finger deep, plant a ruler's length apart. On the front was a photo of a great yellow bloom, a spiraling grid of seeds surrounded by golden feathers. I ripped open the envelope, shook the little skunk-striped teardrops into their palms and imagined our yard, and maybe they did too, full of sunflowers.

One of the boys had white-blonde hair, a little shaggy in the front with freckles across the nose that made him look like

Dennis the Menace or like Ricky Schroder in his Silver Spoons years. He was one of those affectionate kids always curled up and nestled against his mother on the couch, her hand stroking his cheek, tucking stray hair behind his ear. When it was just the two of us—she had a lot of court dates—he'd tell me things.

Every morning before school and then again when I came home until it was dark, he used to make me practice. I had to practice all the time. Saturday, Sunday. It was always tennis, tennis, tennis. My mom said it was too much. I never got to play with any friends 'cause we were always moving, not like moving just always driving to like tournaments and stuff. He had a special shelf for all my trophies. It used to bug me when he'd tell everyone that I was the best player in Canada for the under tens. It's pretty cool, I guess. I kind of just wanted to go fishing sometimes.

He was chatty, an interesting kid, good company. When I took him to see the *Lion King* he asked me, how come the hyenas don't really have a place in the circle of life?

I read in the paper once about a girl from Lebanon whose tears turned to crystal when she cried. Some rare condition called cystinosis caused by a buildup of acid in the body fluids. There was a picture of her, a dark-haired little thing in a headscarf, diamonds glittering in the corners of her eyes. The same article mentioned another weird crying condition called haemolacria where people cry tears of blood. Something about a hormonal imbalance. A thirty-five-year-old woman in the UK lost her job because when the sun got in her eyes at work blood streamed down her face.

Behind the ten-foot-tall opaque wooden fence, we watered and weeded, nurtured the garden. A partial lock-down for a while in late June meant the boys and I could go out in the yard but not in public. The old house was a supposedly secret location, but anything can be found if you're determined enough. Only staff could leave without police escorts and were warned to take precautions. To watch over our shoulders as we walked, to look in the back seats of our cars before opening the doors, to check and double check as we mounted our bikes. Even in daylight we were warned to watch for reflections in windows and rearview mirrors.

Working in a place of crisis isn't for everyone. Working here takes a special kind of person is what the director said during my interview. Special how, is what I should have asked. But I didn't ask. Like always, I just leapt. I'd last leapt into leading canoe trips for youth at risk in Algonquin Park and paddled my way through that just fine, so I figured I'd be all right here too. I guess she thought I was special enough. A minor in Women's Studies didn't hurt but I'm not sure it's helped. Women Studies 101, 201, 301, Women in Religion, Women in Literature, Women in History? I knew about Wicca, Woolf and Wollstonecraft, the suffragists, the 51% minority, the first wave, the second wave, the third wave of feminism. I knew about patriarchy and oppression and inequality in the workplace. I knew about female poverty in the first, second and third worlds. I knew about rape and power and mental illness and what makes pornography sexy. I knew that domestic abuse transcended all races and all socio-economic brackets, that stopping abuse was something we all could get behind, a cause we all shared. I knew why the caged bird sings. But no one told me about men's anger. And no one told me about the boys.

Out from the black earth, came green, double-leafed seedlings that would grow sturdy into knee-high stalks. The boys kept weeding and watering, checking for growth each day. They were excited, protective of their fuzzy plants, protective of their new beginnings.

My mom and him would fight about it. He took me to these courts- near the place at the lake where we were staying- to practice. That's where it happened at that lake near here. You know what happened?

I didn't know. I didn't want to know. I didn't want him to have to say though he should feel free to speak his truth, he should feel safe enough with me to unload the burdens of his ten years. It's just that lately I'd been running out of places to put everybody else's pain.

It was with a knife. And I was screaming and trying to stop him, and my mom was yelling for me to run away but I wouldn't, and he grabbed her and then people came around and then someone called the cops and now we're here. I don't mind. It's ok. I don't mind not playing tennis.

Actually, I really like it, only maybe not all the time, you know?

With my roommate at the grocery store there was a sign. A picture on the community corkboard, a nest of striped kittens, tiny pink noses, skulls the size of tangerines, furry black and grey stripes, whiskers poking out. FREE TO GOOD HOME. Come on, we could do it, I say. Kittens become cats, she says.

Boys become men. Men become lovers and fathers and husbands. What kind of men will these boys become? Who will teach these boys to be men?

The over-night crisis worker waved at me from the window of the front office as I came into work. She was on the phone and rolled her eyes and mouthed the word crazy. But I could tell what kind of morning it had been from the sound of her voice when she buzzed me through. Two new women sat behind the glass in the smoking room. I smiled and waved at them as I crossed through the kitchen toward my office at the back of the house. The one with her arm in a sling turned toward me and nodded. The side of her face was purple and swollen, a bloody spider web of cuts across her cheeks. The other one had a fat lip with a dark red crust and a missing tooth.

I stared at my Nalgene bottle. Then my colleague came in and tossed a folder in front of me on the desk. Five new child profiles in the folder, all boys. God, she said throwing her hands up. It just never stops. We had one woman in the hospital all night getting shards of glass picked out of her face; the guy shoved her head right through a window.

We planted a garden, we swam, we played basketball and baseball, soccer, went for walks, made crayon etchings from the gravestones in the cemetery. Truth is, I'm easily bored—what else could we do outside on a limited budget? Fish? And so, with borrowed fishing rods and reels, a donated box of old tackle, we went fishing, the five boys and me, at the creek by the canal at the end of the lake. A place full of weeds where pike would hide and dart in among the water lilies' roots. Pink and white and yellow lilies floating there, belonging to no one, and looking like something Monet would like to paint, or like lotuses maybe.

Each boy chose a lure from the box and stood there trying not to hook his own fingers as he waited for his turn, for me to teach him, like my dad taught me, how to tie the line.

Lower now, cast it, watch out, don't stand so close to each other, careful! Good for you!

I got one! I got one! What do I do! What do I do?

Easy now, gently, slowly, carefully. Don't want to hurt it, kindly, tenderly, ease it out. Fishing with a vegetarian. I pass them a pair of yellow rubber kitchen gloves.

No way! You do it! Gross! I can't.

So, I pull on the gloves and squeeze the fish to stop it flipping this way and that. Gently unhook the barb, slowly remove it, kindly, carefully, slip it back into the water.

When I was running up the subway steps after dinner with some friends the other day, a man in a suit with one of those old-fashioned briefcases ran up ahead of me. He had on red and blue nylon socks, at least I thought he did, then I realized his socks were more like tights and went up underneath the legs of his suit pants. I wondered if he was looking for a phone booth. I wondered if he knew how badly he was needed.

The sunflowers were growing taller with big broad leaves like a jungle tree. The little ones couldn't believe the plants had outgrown them and would pretend to hide under their sheltering fronds as the afternoon sun shone down upon them and no one thought to hide their smiles.

When they call looking for me, the tennis boy and his beautiful blonde mother, the counselor who takes the call recommends not maintaining ties with former clients. But they want me to come for dinner. His mother with heavily accented words says, we must thank you. It feels disingenuous not to accept. The trial is over, the man is in jail, they are safe.

It's just a small, simple apartment, oatmeal walls, one single mattress upon the living room floor. They've retrieved some clothes and personal effects, but the mother-in-law intervened and would not let them take any furniture. Where a table might have been, there's a tablecloth spread out picnic style, laid with mismatched dishes, a poster by the kitchen of yellow abstract flowers. And I see, as I get closer that the tablecloth is checkered with neat rows of sunflowers. She watches me looking, says, I love sunflowers. I smile and say, me too, wondering if she remembers those seeds we planted six weeks ago or was she just too buried in life to notice.

She presses play, the smooth sounds of Barry White rise and fall around us crackling out from an old grey tape player. She apologizes. I love music, she says, but only have the one cassette. Here's my bean salad, I say, thanks for having me. Plump, fried chicken, three pieces on a plate, drops of oil pooling underneath. It must have cost her a fortune. I've not eaten chicken in ten years, but I eat that chicken.

You are so kind, she says. No, I say and then, thank you. Yes, she says, and hands me a small white jewelry box. No, I say, I couldn't. The boy's eyes expectant. Inside, layered in folds of cotton, a pair of earrings. Large earrings, silver and turquoise. These were my favourite earrings, she says, when I was young like you and liked to dance. Take, take. She presses them at me no matter my protestations. I hold them up to my ears and imagine her dancing in a European nightclub, house music thumping, sweat on the upper lip of her smooth, pink-cheeked skin.

The sunflowers are up to my shoulders. Even the women take a break from crying and smoking and talking and cooking to have a look at them. The buds are still green and hang from the stalks like fists. Someone's mother smiles at me, takes my hand and shakes her head at my uneven, bitten nails. I can do these up for you, if you want, she says. Her nails are long and mauve with black stars. That'd be cool, I say.

In the driveway, once the partial lockdown is lifted, we play basketball and chalk. Some neighbourhood kids ride by on bikes shouting, Welfare cases! Rejects! The house is not that secret. A fifteen-year-old lawyer's son who I'm almost beating at HORSE drops the ball, tells me he's going in to watch TV. The younger boys ask what them kids said. Ask, why'd he say welfare, what's that mean? I say it means he has a bigger mouth than he has a brain. But no one wants to chalk any more.

After the Labour Day weekend, the boys are off to school. I rush straight through the house to the window at the back hoping to see if those green fists opened into flowers.

A dented red snow shovel across the dirt. A hockey stick. Stalks hacked down, broken on the lawn, stalks bent in half, buds sweeping at the dirt.

Maybe sunflowers are too much to ask for, maybe sunflowers are only safe when tucked away inside our minds, something that grows on the other side of the glass. Maybe, when you're afraid to go to sleep at night, sunflowers can only exist in the abstract.

I've never worn those earrings. It's not that I don't like them, they're precious. I take them out of my jewelry box some-times, touch the dangling silver sticks with the turquoise stones, hear the melodic tones of Barry White and think of little boys, of windows, of sunflowers and then I tuck them back inside the folds of cotton.

ZUG
ZWANG

Zugzwang

"Mating," he said, sipping a non-descript red from plastic stemware, "checkmating in particular, is the *objective* though not the *essence* of the game."

"I've just been for Chinese," she said, slurping the rest of her wine. "According to this placemat's birth chart I'm a tiger who'd have an auspicious pairing with a horse, a dragon, or a pig. When were you born?"

"November." He raised a finger. "Actually, *threats* and *tempo* are the *essence* of a chess game. It's the threat of loss that fuels or inspires the tempo with which each move is made."

"Month and year." She juggled her empty wine glass and unfolded a damp placemat ringed with drink stains.

"November 1976." When Callum leaned forward to help the lithe, curly haired stranger flatten the paper mat so that she could better interpret her dates, his forearm brushed against hers and he unwittingly inhaled. As involuntary as synapses firing, as subliminal as a wet dream, he envisioned handholding, felt the sensation of tongue on tongue, the tang of warm, moist female flesh. He watched as she dragged her pink fingernail down the list of years, forgetting entirely about his lame attempt to answer her question as to the point or purpose of a game like chess.

"1976. That makes you a dragon!" She poked the compatibility chart next to the animal descriptions.

He swept a dark lock from his forehead and asked this newly enchanting Paula if she would like more wine.

She grasped at his shoulder and turned the plastic glass upside down. "Callum, that's your name, right? I can't drink any more of this plonk. But since we're fated compatible, I might be persuaded to have a real drink somewhere else."

She'd only graced this faculty party as a favour to her physics undergraduate friend and now that he was enthralled with another student by the cheese tray, she was off the hook.

Delighted by her insolence and her willingness to drink a little too much in light of the night's pretensions, though he would later learn this sort of behaviour was not often repeated, Callum agreed. Nodded and winked to a fellow PhD candidate and pointed Paula towards the exit. Said, "There's a pub on the corner two blocks up." The promise of wet, drunk, pheromonal kisses from a dancer trumped a faculty pissing match any day. Chess, like lust, was a game between kings and queens where anything could happen.

"The king," he said, "is the most important piece but is vulnerable and possesses little power. He has limited movement and spends most of his time in protective custody. The queen, conversely, with her unlimited movement is the most powerful. She can even create allies, as pawns may become queens to assist in taking down a king."

"It sounds to me," said Paula, "that queens risk it all while kings have limited potential and spend most of their time backed into a corner." And, without pausing for reaction, without a seeming whit of care for her companion's ego or genius she turned to the server and ordered a pint. "I've been thinking about the look of a chessboard, all those squares of light and dark."

"Thirty-two light, Thirty-two dark."

"Right. The light doesn't necessarily have to be in opposition to the dark, it doesn't automatically mean they must be pitted against each other." She produced the damp placement, pointed to a circular yin-yang on the upper right corner. "Harmony: the necessary presence of both. Without dark there is no light. Without female there is no male. Without evil there is no good. Without death there is no life. Without moon there is no sun."

And on this way their conversations, their relationship continued like two parallel lines never seeming to intersect.

An old man in an indiscreet white and blue speckled hospital gown shuffles past Paula, carping about having waited two hours with a full bladder to get his prostate examined. A nurse from X-ray and imaging responds to his gripe: "We've had a busy day, sir, we're at least two hours behind." A collective sigh from the waiting room resounds. They have started her 'pit drip' and left her here on the stretcher in the east wing hallway on the second floor to spare her the wailing of newborns on the maternity ward while the wonders of modern medicine work their nefarious magic. Along the length of the cream brick wall there is a mural of small handprints. Pink. Yellow. Mauve. Aqua. Repeat. Each seemed to drip a two-leafed green stem from its centre.

As though her eyes were tiny, clenched fists, she pummels back the present looping through her brain. Reminds herself to be grateful for all that she has. Wills herself into memory. It is their wedding day at her parents' orchard. The sun reflects promise off white circus tents. Inside, steel pails of tall pink glads flank entrances, and food-laden platters encourage friends and family to gather round and celebrate. Usually so confident and verbose, Callum had barely been able to say that he'd love, honour, and cherish Paula all the days of her life. The tenderness inside him so rarely shown, now displayed for all. A perfect day, a perfect glimpse into their future marred only by a single incident.

Callum's friend Stephen chauffeured the newlyweds to their bed and breakfast, not far from the orchard gathering. Jovial, until a thud, clear as if they had crested a log of firewood, rose up from underneath Stephen's Civic. Paula demanded they stop because she knew, she just knew. Hiked up her wedding dress and trudged toward the furry bump roadside and saw that it was a porcupine, its protective spikes useless against their car. Saw the chest of the beast rising and falling asthmatically. "We need something heavy," she shouted.

Stephen grabbed an old snow shovel from his trunk and stood with Callum looking at it, and at her, as she bludgeoned the dying animal. The two of them flinched. She'd only wanted to put it out of its misery. They drove on in silence, with Paula leaning forward from the backseat, draping her arms around Callum's shoulders in an effort to console him that the night was not spoiled, all the while conscious of the fresh splatter of blood on white silk.

Someone dressed in white rushes past. A wet mop sloshes across the polished concrete. Antiseptic lemon wafts up from the mopping and jars her back into the hospital vortex. She was always doing this. She wished she could isolate the brain cells responsible for such activity and pop them like bubble wrap. She'd been thinking about gratitude and what a lovely day it had been and now all she can do is conjure that murderous episode of porcupine bashing. It felt as though she'd been rotting here for hours. When would they move her from this hallway purgatory? It must surely be time to transfer her to the operating or delivery or whatever they call it kind of room and get this *procedure* underway.

Time. Tempo. Time could torture. And tempo is the essence of a chess game, no, not just tempo, tempo and threats, that's what Callum would say. Bless his faint heart, always keeping himself once removed, hiding behind metaphors and playing at life through his chessboard.

He was a man wed to planning, to directives and deliverables, solutions to every problem. Paula, less so. Though she was known in certain circles for her ability to dance with precise movement and elegant classical form, she preferred the undulating rhythms and sweeping lyrical gestures of modern dance. They'd been living in Toronto the past six years while Callum taught and researched at a variety of area universities. He insisted on contraception until he had secured tenure, until they owned a home. She waited fulfilling herself in the meantime by performing with a contemporary dance company and instructing at a downtown studio with a former university colleague. Paula understood, to a certain extent, that strategy had its limits. She knew that yin and yang would occasionally bleed into grey.

They had stared with parental wonder as the technician used blue jelly and a transducer wand to divine the image of their offspring orbiting inside of Paula. A contrast of silver spine and alien skull against the blackness of her womb. They laughed with the technician as she pointed out the head, arms, legs, and feet. And

Callum kissed Paula's mouth, solidifying their shared joy at the mystery of their little one coming into being through the dance of love.

"Today is one of the safest times to have a baby." Dr. Macmillan assuaged their fears with his great white wisdom as he examined the results of their initial ultrasound, and they crossed successfully the threshold of their first trimester. "You've reached the earliest milestone, many pregnancies end in miscarriage before twelve weeks, nature's selection." She and Callum had relaxed. It was settled by fate.

There was something different, though, about the technician's demeanor at the twenty-week ultrasound. This one's eyebrows narrowed as she scrutinized the monitor. Had not been able to take her eyes off the screen. "I can't answer your questions," she said, "I'm not a doctor, but he should have the results in three business days." Business days? Checks cleared on business days, not babies. Next day at the studio, Paula got an urgent message from Dr. Macmillan's secretary. Called Callum and scurried across town to the doctor's office. Multiple abnormalities had been detected. An amniocentesis was booked for Thursday at 9:00 and a meeting with a genetic counselor scheduled.

During the amnio, they watched the nurse transduce their baby from womb to screen. Callum rested his hand on her shoulder and stared alternately between the ultrasound monitor and Paula's swollen belly. Dr. Wu wiped yellow liquid across her middle and administered a numbing shot that required several minutes to take effect. When Dr. Wu returned, he carried with him a hollow, elongated needle. It was hard for Paula to imagine that a person's body could survive penetration by such a device. Dr. Wu dismissed concerns in sketchy English and reamed his steel proboscis into her abdomen. The nurse held her hand, encouraged her to look up at the pictures of sunsets, monarch butterflies, Caribbean bound sailboats ripped from a drugstore calendar and scotch-taped to the ceiling. To her left, a fetal astronaut, navigating its nascent world. To her right, the worried face of Callum wondering, perhaps, how the rules could change when he knew every defense in the book.

They had argued over names for months. Callum insisted the child be named in homage to his Scottish heritage. Invoked the middle name of his paternal great-grandmother in hopes of winning her over. But to Paula, names like Magnus, Alistair, Elspeth and Agnes reeked of sensible shoes, cabbage and unwanted body hair. She preferred names with romance and cadence: Leander (lion like) or Phoebe (bright, shining, moon). And always she had asked what kind of world am I bringing my child into, never had she thought to ask what kind of child am I bringing into this world.

The genetic counselor reported the amniocentesis results. The fetus was female and had a chromosomal abnormality called Trisomy 13 or Patau's Syndrome. She opened a three-ringed binder across the table, flipped to a karyotype, pointed to the presence of an extra chromosome on number thirteen.

In the beginning there are 23 incomplete pairs seeking a match to expand and become 46. Flipped, there are 64, the number of squares on the chessboard. What use would a chessboard be with one extra square, Callum wondered.

"Given the nature of such abnormalities," the counselor said, "the prognosis of the fetus should you decide to carry to term would be what we refer to as *incompatible with life*. Eighty percent of trisomy babies die within one month of birth." She flipped the page to reveal pictures and bulleted lists of aberrations: webbing, holey hearts, underdeveloped livers, incomplete lungs, fused eyes. Babies who had lived mere hours with a single cyclopean orb glowering in the shadow of grotesque triple flaps masquerading as nostrils. "According to the genetic charts we created based on your histories, this incident is one of chance. Suppose you might say your probability of such a disorder is like winning the lottery. At this point, "she bravely continued while eying the karyotypes, "if you choose to terminate the pregnancy measures must be taken immediately." She excused herself, leaving them to their bright, shining Phoebe, to the binder of monstrosities and to their judgment.

Callum looked into Paula's moist eyes and without expression said, "It's a zugzwang."

Paula's face, as if a queen's carved of wood, stared back.

"You know," he said, "a German chess term for compulsion to move. Being forced into a position of greater threat."

Months ahead of her due date, with knees raised, Paula reclines on the gurney in the delivery room. She caresses her round middle, thinking of the phrase *incompatible with life*. Thinking of the black and white swirl of yin yang, thinking without death there is no life, without moon there is no sun. That flaw is just perfection's complement. And like the tide, constant at the mercy of the moon, she allows herself to deliver from hollow darkness radiance complete.

SOME
KID

Some Kid

Tamara stood looking out at the mass of students in the lecture hall. It would be a year before she again commanded this stage, and she wasn't going to miss teaching World Literature to first years one bit. She walked her huge, pregnant self over to her computer to pull up the various artworks, visual companions, to her lecture on Ovid's *Metamorphoses*. Her steps echoed over the hard wood. She still wore heels despite having finally admitted that her feet hurt and that she wouldn't be wearing them again until this baby was out, if all went according to plan, and she couldn't think of a reason why it wouldn't. The cesarian had been scheduled months in advance due to concerns about her too-small pelvis and her giant-headed, nearly seven-foot-tall husband. Once she'd linked the computer and the smart board with the remote and had the image of a Greek Vase depicting the weaving war between Minerva and Arachne, she began her lecture with a recap of book six.

She walked over to the chalk board as she spoke, aware of the growing girth of her feet pressing into the sides of her beloved shoes. She knew it was stupid by anyone's standards to wear such unsensible footwear while pregnant, but she just wasn't ready to give up. She refused to let this impending child change who she was—Tamara—accomplished, talented, intelligent, stylish wife of the quasi-famous documentary film maker, David Ireland. Not some matronly frumpadump toting a mewling infant on her hip while wearing sweatpants and Crocs. She could still be Professor Tamara Becker and a mother. She didn't have to let it all go. She poked through the chalk shelf with a red fingernail until she found the longest piece then wrote and drew circles and arrows and double underlines as she lectured.

"If we think back to Ovid's opening verses on creation, he writes about the pre-existing chaos. Everything is made of chaos and Ovid speaks more of ordering this chaos than of creating something from nothing. So, if we look at it this way, it is less a story of creation and more one of imposing a shape or a framework to organize and order the everchanging, unstable, shifting shapeless mass that is chaos. Yes?" Murmurs and nods from the audience. "And therefore, in these stories of metamorphoses there is constant transformation: nothing stays the same. We have Daphne and Phaeton's sisters turned into trees, Dianna's handmaid into a bear, we've got bats, and gorgons and spiders, well you all remember, you've all read it right?" She looked at the class and raised her eyebrows suggestively. She suspected half of them were counting on her to fill them in, connect all the proverbial dots rather than do the work themselves. Anyway, they'd be Gareth's problem now. It was her last day before maternity leave. Perfectly timed. Wouldn't be back until next September. She continued: "We get the feeling, I think, that maybe Ovid is a little less than pious. No? In fact, at times, he's downright irreverent. He shows the gods behaving like people, like children really, because there are no consequences. A woman transforms into a tree on a whim. And, overall, mortal women become pawns for the sexual escapades of the Gods, the rape of Europa by Jupiter, for example. They become involved in the affairs of the mortals, as well, which isn't really very god-like or dignified, given they think so little of petty humans." She maneuvered herself over to the screen with the first picture, the Greek vase, and reminded the class that Minerva is the Roman equivalent of Athena, goddess of wisdom, war, and handicraft. She clicked to the next slide, Velasquez's painting of the contest. "So here we have the lovely and talented, Arachne, who, despite her humble origins as the daughter of a weaver and man who made a name for himself by dying cloth a glorious shade of purple, has achieved relative fame for her artistic weaving: one of the few ways in which women were permitted to be creative. The problem arises when she brags that she is not only not indebted to Minerva for her skills, but that she is better than

Minerva even, as a weaver. Well, you can imagine how Minerva feels about this sort of hubris from a mortal. She disguises herself as an old woman and demands that Arachne recant her boast. Arachne, stubborn, arrogant, and passionate about her art, will not. The challenge for 'who wove it best' ensues. Now what is important is not just the aesthetic qualities of the tapestries, but rather what these woven images represent. Minerva has shown the gods and goddesses in benevolence, triumph, and majesty (Neptune riding the waves, Jupiter with his thunderbolts and the like). In the other corner of the ring, we have Ms. Arachne who has artfully scolded the gods by depicting them in a less than favourable light. Rapes, thefts, transformations with the intention of trickery etc."

Tamara flipped to the next slide, Robusti's painting of the weaving. "On top of this insolent insult to Minerva and all gods, is the fact that because of the movement and colour and perfection of her work, Arachne wins the tapestry duel. Enraged, Minerva touches Arachne's forehead causing such shame, she hangs herself, only to be spared at the eleventh hour by Minerva's pity. In the spirit of Ovid's *Metamorphoses*, she transforms Arachne into a spider so that she and all her descendants would be condemned to weave for eternity." Clicked to the image from Dore's illustration in the *Divine Comedy* where Arachne becomes a monstrous, hairy she-spider. Gareth, Tamara's replacement, arrived. Sporting a green V-neck sweater, tan slacks and a leather messenger bag, he fidgeted, as always, with his black sixties-style glasses pushing them up on his nose. He was in dire need of a haircut, or was mid-way to a man bun, and this made him seem boyish even though he and Tamara were both in their early thirties. He nodded to her and sat off to the side with his laptop. She continued, "I wanted to highlight this story as it is an excellent springboard for a discussion of transformation, illusion, deception, power, love, art, violence, arrogance, gender, and even censorship. I will however, at this point, be turning the class over to my substitute as I will be busy forming my shapeless mass into a baby and transforming myself into a mother. Without further ado, here is the most lovely and competent Mr. Lester to help unpack the thematic relevance of *The Metamorphoses*." Gareth tipped an imaginary hat at her and began his lecture.

She heard him etch on the chalk board as he spoke: "Thematically, we have creation vs imitation, Gods versus mortals, master versus pupil, nature versus art, art versus power." She smiled. Wouldn't have to think about any of that for a whole year. When she got to her office, she removed her shoes padding around in stocking feet, and gathering a few personal items, a wedding photo, her journal, an unread copy of *Infinite Jest*, a potted pink orchid in full bloom. The desk was so clear now it was almost as though she had never inhabited this space. She had, effectively, disappeared herself from academia. It was all ready for Gareth to stack and shuffle papers, to slop coffee over everything leaving unsightly, sticky rings. Should she leave something, a pen, a book, a mug, a trace of her old self behind? Penny poked her head through the doorway.

"Look at you. You look like a ripe berry about to burst!" She took the box from Tamara and the two walked down the hall toward the faculty lounge. Penny said she needed to grab her lunch from the fridge, steering Tamara inside where she was met by a resounding SURPRISE from all available Humanities and English faculty. The room smelled of fresh coffee. There were purple, yellow, and green balloons floating along the ceiling their long-ribboned tails dangling down in a curtain of celebration the likes of which the faculty lounge of beige and brown had never seen. There were also traditional baby shower balloons of pink and blue that read *it's a girl* and *it's a boy* over which someone had Sharpied, replacing the gendered epitaphs, with: it's a human, it's a person. Red wine flowed into plastic stemware. Tamara tasted it in her imagination and could hardly wait until she could once again participate in such festivities. Pat, of magenta hair and turquoise cat's-eye glasses, had gone to a lot of trouble to get the cake, she explained. On the large table, laden with brightly packaged baby themed gifts, sat front and centre, an enormous sheet cake. On one side of the confection was a grotesque baby head squeezing out of a pink icing labium covered in pubic hair fashioned from chocolate curls and sprinkles. On the other side in cursive: *Congratulations on using your genitals to make a baby.* Tamara took several photos to share with David. It had to be seen to be believed. Penny guided her to a chair decorated with bows and ribbons of every colour and handed her some sort of fruit juice cocktail with an umbrella. Professors Nolan and Sweet were quibbling over the superiority of Christopher Marlowe and Ben Jonson to Shakespeare. "Can you imagine?" said Penny with a wink, "You're not going to see this bunch for a whole year!"

A whole year. Tamara beamed.

"What will you do with yourself? You should write a novel or put together a new book of your poems!"

"Well, I imagine the baby will take up some of my time," she patted her belly, "other than that, I plan to relax and I'm finally going to have time to read this." She reached into the box from her office and pulled out *Infinite Jest.*

"Overrated," said Penny. "Here, open mine first." She handed Tamara a gift bag frothing with yellow tissue paper and covered in photos of old-fashioned baby shoes. People didn't make their babies wear those nowadays, did they? What Tamara didn't know about babies could fill this faculty lounge and here she was, last day of work before, well, different work, she supposed. Tomorrow she would have a creature of her own to look after. She wasn't even "delivering" the kid so much as having it removed. Panic welled inside her but was instantly overshadowed by her annoyance at Horace Nolan who remarked:

"I can't even imagine having a year to myself, what a luxury."

"It's called maternity leave, Horace, not a vacation," said Penny.

"Of course, things were different for me, back in those days, my wife had the children and made a home for our family, while I came here. Now it would seem you can do both. Is it any better for the children though, I wonder?"

"You can always retire," said Penny who then rolled her eyes and said to Tamara, "You know what they say about tenure," and here Tamara chimed in, "it means never having to say you're sorry."

"Go on! Open it!" Tamara pulled out a glass and silver framed embroidery with the text of Dr. Seuss's, *Oh the Places You'll Go.* Next to *Charlotte's Web,* it was Tamara's favourite children's story. A fitting gift from a professor of Children's Literature. She read the first few phrases aloud and reached up to hug Penny thanking her profusely for her time and effort. She seemed almost more excited about the baby than Tamara. Horace, having moved on, shared his coffee-wine breath along with his thoughts on Beowulf and Grendel with some other poor soul. Penny was having none of it: "Horace, Tamara is about to have a baby, Grendel can wait." She turned to Tamara and said quietly, "that sounds like the title of a romantic comedy, or a sitcom or something, Grendel Can Wait. And he's this big, ugly, Olympic shot putter trying to make his way in the world and every time he's embroiled in some kind of romantic escapade his overbearing mother interferes. Sorry, sorry, next present!" Penny plopped an enormous pink, tissue paper bon-bon in her lap. Tamara eventually left her baby shower exhausted, overwhelmed by the generosity of her colleagues. When she arrived home, David was there chopping garlic and stuffing lemons inside of a whole raw chicken. He unloaded the car, helped her to the sofa, placed the orchid on the glass coffee table, dragged the ottoman under her feet, ran a hot bath, and settled Tamara into it with a mug of vanilla chamomile tea.

"Savour this moment," he said, "this is the last day of life as we know it."

She sank down into the tub, her pregnant belly rising from the water like an island. No, like a volcano. A volcano about to erupt and empty leaving all around it altered, her former self a curled-up, ash covered Pompeian.

David sat with her a while, kissed her forehead, trailed a soapy washcloth across her middle and then let her be while he carried on with dinner. She loved that he was so excited, it was all so exciting. And scary. A surgeon was cutting open layers of her body tomorrow. With, like, a knife. A sharp one. Through muscle, skin, organs, her womb. What if he went too deep and cut the baby's foot off? Ok, that was just stupid. Would her stomach ever go back to normal, or would she have a big floppy apron of skin like a formerly obese person? And what about the potential for paralysis with the spinal epidural? Stop, she told herself, stop. As nervous as she was for the procedure tomorrow, she was also anxious to have this baby out. The months of deprivation, no wine, no coffee, no brie, the weeping, the stretch marks, the swollen, tender breasts, the hemorrhoids, the feeling of walking bow legged with a bowling ball between her legs for the last month. The ugly maternity clothes. Waddling around like a manatee out of water tottering on her fat feet stuffed into her favourite heels. Flatulence and heart burn. Get this kid out! It was a bit like unleashing something, though, a Pandora's Box situation, all the ills of the world that can never be put back. No, no, no, a new baby was unleashing good things. God, she hoped so. What if she had a kid like Kevin in, *We Need to Talk about Kevin*? Fiction, pure fiction. What about those Columbine kids? Those poor mothers. The guy who shot up l'École Polytechnique? Stop, stop, stop! It would all be over tomorrow. It would all start tomorrow. Tomorrow, she would become somebody's mother.

The first month, although a whirlwind, she at least had David around to help. Of course, he made a pest of himself by filming her slow cesarian recovery, her hunched over robed walks to the bathroom, her wincing fear of sneezing and undoing all the staples that held her abdomen together, and all the other intimate moments of their new life as a family. She had learned to endure living with a documentarian. At least he could keep an eye on baby Joshua while she made a sandwich or had a shower. But since he's been back to work, Tamara was having to make all sorts of adjustments: eating when Joshua slept, securing him into the portable car seat when she bathed. When she looked in the mirror, she saw her same bloated pregnancy face, only now it looked haggard from sleeplessness. Her torso, draped in David's grey waffle-knit shirt to accommodate her massive, always leaking tits, betrayed two big wet spots blooming like something gross in a petri dish. This bit of motherhood was a terrible inheritance.

Tamara sat cross-legged on the sofa looking out the window, a tiny beast in her lap sucking on her breasts. When he finished with one, she'd switch him to the other. It made her think of the shops lining Little Portugal advertising suckling pig and those piglets, pink and wet looking, hanging up by their hooves. She picked up *Infinite Jest* and began reading the first paragraph. She returned it to the coffee table. Reached instead for *What to Expect the First Year,* every milestone marked in daily, monthly increments. She would just get used to one thing, it would seem, before he would be doing something else. She flipped to the index in the back. Dragged a finger down the b column looking for boredom. Then isolation. Then ennui. Nothing. She was stuck here watching the world go on without her through the window like some kind of matronly Emily Dickinson.

Everyone she knew was busy at work. She spoke to Penny on the phone once and she'd kindly filled her in on all expected faculty banality. Had enjoyed good old CBC radio for a while until she tired of the same news and traffic every half hour. She had thought this whole *maternity leave* thing would be more fun. Puttering around and baking muffins. Wearing yoga pants and commiserating with other moms. Maybe she wasn't cut out for motherhood. Now, if someone needed an essay written, that she could do. Quick! Grab the *Norton Anthology* stat! She didn't even like muffins. What kind of a monster didn't like muffins? Clearly, she needed to get out of the house. The kid was after all, nearly three months old and her body had healed enough from the surgery to walk about safely. She'd take the kid and grab a few groceries. Her mind was mush, couldn't remember a damn thing. She'd have to make a list. Took a Post-it and jotted down what she needed. And now that Joshua was fed, the last thing to do before buckling him in the car seat and leaving, was a clean diaper.

She laid him on the change table and opened his diaper. Suddenly, explosive diarrhea ricocheted across the room and all over the changing pad, all over the cute little basket that held the wipes, all over her. Oh, dear God—not the wicker. There was excrement everywhere. In her flurry to wipe dark yellow, curdled breast milk from between the folds of his bottom, she hadn't noticed that his jaws were moving, that he was gumming something, and saliva had accumulated at his mouth corners. She couldn't possibly stick her shit covered hands inside his mouth giving him E. coli or something. She scrubbed them with baby wipes, and sweeping a little finger inside his mouth, retrieved part of the grocery list: just a bite of moistened yellow paper with the ink blurred. She plunged her finger in again scoping between the gums but was ultimately unable to retrieve the missing piece of Post-it. He hadn't choked. He didn't seem to be poisoned. She reprimanded herself her maternal failings. The baby babbled. It sounded more of a chuckle. Instead of venturing out, Tamara slumped into the sofa and watched a Facebook video someone she hadn't seen since elementary school had posted about fainting goats. The way they walked normally until startled and then instantly fell over, amused her to no end. It was kind of sick, really, how entertaining she found this genetic mutation.

The next time she changed his diaper, before David arrived home, something strange happened. She opened the diaper and there, glistening between his buttocks, was the piece of paper he had swallowed. It wasn't chewed, he didn't have teeth so that checked out, but wouldn't the digestive acids have done something to it? It was crumpled, it had been through… something… and there was, of course, feces smeared on and coating it, but she could still make out a single word: DREAM. Tamara was certain that DREAM wasn't on her shopping list, had she written cream? Of course, not! She had all this baby weight to lose. Buying full fat dairy, how absurd. DREAM? She must be overly tired, baby brain, fogged by exhaustion and hormones. Should she show David? Probably not. He'd think she'd cracked. She blotted off the intestinal residue with a collection of tissues and wipes and puzzled about what to do with the evidence. Tucked the Post-it with the pooped-out DREAM between the pages of her journal wondering where the other words had gone.

Later that week, Tamara decided to take Joshua to the library for a children's program she'd read about in the insert that came along with the grocery flyer that arrived every Thursday. Yes: she was reduced to anticipating and reading the grocery flyers, *Infinite Jest* be damned. She had tried some of the other mommy and me classes that entailed insipid conversations with other mothers about babies and sleeping and breast milk and food and bodily functions and simply could not bear them. She'd take a conversation with Horace over those any day and held on hope that the library offering would be different. She secured the baby in place on the changing table pressing gently on his red belly with the length of her fingers. His eyes darted back and forth following the purposely stimulating black and white optical illusion mobile that spun in hypnotizing circles she had put in her baby registry hoping to steer him along his certain route to genius. The Velcro tear of the reusable diaper tab that Tamara ripped open startled him. He quivered, looked at his mother and cooed. She smiled. Felt layers of love unfolding within her like the petals of a lush rose slowly opening in stop motion. She could picture the image in one of David's documentary openings, a metaphor revealing the centre point of all life's purpose. How could anyone who's never had a child ever feel such a depth of love, thought Tamara. Then, finding herself back at ground zero, she clutched today's Post-it on which she had written a single word, MOTHER. She held the note between thumb and forefinger, enticingly, she supposed, over the child's head as she grabbed both feet with the other hand and slipped the wet diaper out from underneath him. He snatched the list mid change and stuffed it in his mouth.

That evening, Tamara was astonished to find in his diaper amongst the curds and mustard, the very piece of paper that had disappeared into his gullet earlier that day. On it, was the word transformed to read: *if the thread be one of love, there is no wrong way to weave.* What in the name of Clarissa Dalloway? Where had all those extra words come from? Her son was a genius. She must tell everyone. The world deserved to know! Perhaps her son was akin to that literary spider of her youth, Charlotte. How delightful. But who could she tell? The retired couple who lives to the left of them? Knock on the door, lead with, it's kind of a funny story. Or you'll never guess what I found in my son's diaper! It's not like there were any community newspapers or a county fair anymore. Friends? Family? The grocery store clerk? The librarian? She, of all people, would understand. But would she? There was, after all, the small matter of the manner in which the messages arrived. How very McLuhan-esque. She sanitized the rumpled Post-it and slipped it into the journal next to the first, still afraid to actually tell anyone what had happened lest they believe her to have taken leave of her senses. But she hadn't, while frazzled, she still had all her marbles in fairly decent, sometimes hormonally charged, but still sane, condition.

The incident, however, would not abate. When he got home, she reluctantly explained what had happened to David even going so far as to show him the Post-its. God, what had she been thinking? She really was, as her husband said, losing her fucking mind. Bats in the belfry. Away with the fairies to Bedlam.

She would prove her sanity with a third Post-it on which she had scrawled, RADIANT. She felt just like Templeton the rat. She squatted on the floor and played with Joshua, who sat in a special chair that promised to sturdy his spine, offering an assortment of intelligence boosting board books and nesting shape games. While the baby seemed content to gnaw on the head of a rubber giraffe, excitement fizzled beneath the surface of Tamara's skin like bubbles in the veins of a junkie just waiting to float to her brain and stroke her out with an airy embolism. Then on cue, she heard the rumbling and smelled the tell-tale scent of success. Sure enough, the child laughed and shat out a new phrase: *everything changes, nothing is lost.* Calloo callay! He had done it again. She hadn't fallen off her rocker. But if he was Charlotte wouldn't that make her Wilbur?

She imagined sitting next to Ellen having a humorous conversation about the amazing creature she had birthed. Her social media feeds would be a twitter with brilliant, poetic gems penned (?) by her offspring. She should start a blog! Word Weaver, or Shit my Son Says, or Shit my Son Shits? Well, something like that. There would be feel-good news story segments, the talk show circuit. Oprah! They'd be famous. Except for the fact that a good portion of the story involved defecation.

If only he could do it without first shuttling it through his colon. It would be so much more palatable. Easier for the public to digest.

She called Penny. Approached the topic gently, hinting that her son had shown fantastical promise in literature, but Penny wouldn't bite. Had asked, in fact, if she'd thought about hiring help and maybe returning to work a little early. How could she know anything about motherhood and the love of one's child? But the more Tamara thought about it, the more she felt deeply unsuited to this life of sloppiness. Not to mention that her mind was eating itself.

In any case, the lure of fame from her son's unique abilities had her compose and dangle a fourth Post-it, a laundry list of her very most personal desires above his expectant mouth. She'd probably have to get him an agent. Devote her life to developing his talent. Or maybe Penny was right. She scrolled her phone for various supports: childcare, cleaning, a nanny service. It didn't hurt to look.

Shortly thereafter, Joshua did not disappoint, producing from his feces a magical yellow Post-it:

The dragonfly moults

Through illusion accepting

Iridescent wings

My God, thought Tamara, my son has shat out a haiku! He was Basho, and Rumi, and Charlotte, and Ram Dass all rolled into one. What was next? A tanka? That was some kid she had. Some kid.

She glanced at the coffee table. Her joy faded. The lovely pink orchid that had been in full bloom when she'd brought it home had now wizened. She took a closer look. The flowers were gone. The green stems dry, a root poked up and appeared mouldy. How had she managed to kill something by simultaneously over and under watering? She tried to smooth the jagged edge of her fingernail with her tooth. Gnawed off a piece of a hang nail. Surely chaos could not be ordered with poetry.

And yet.

HARD
TO
SWALLOW

Hard to Swallow

Wish I could say we met in Paris in the springtime at a café. Or something dreamy and romantic like that. Maybe in the future, I'll reinvent the story that way after time has soothed the sting, and frequent repetition has skewed so many details that truth is just the skeleton and fattened-up fiction the flesh. Like that time in Venice, ages ago. I tell people I partied with gondoliers until five a.m. I neglect to add, however, that I got pissed on cheap Spumanti by eleven, puked out the side of the gondola by twelve, and passed out in the boat until their return from the party at five. And I could tell them all about me and Will falling in love while working as art instructors at a camp in upstate New York, but I'd be afraid of fudging the specifics. Besides, cheerful beginnings, never mind the falsified details, seem to be what people want to hear, though it's miserable endings, with their indelible clarity, I seem to remember best.

After everything, he tells me he doesn't love her, has never loved her. While we sat warm and satisfied, climatically speaking, in a red velvet cocktail lounge somewhere in Bumblefuck, New York, and I ate the pickle from my Bloody Mary, which at the time I thought an odd garnish to put in a drink, having been weaned on celery-sticked Caesars in small-town Ontario. I saw a smudge of green paint on my calf, and like a fool touched it, surprised at its longevity, that it could survive our hotel room rollick. How paint could feel so raw and wet though it had been hours since we'd painted the mural with all the art instructors commemorating the end of another successfully survived camp season without incident or death. Well, almost. I took the damp napkin from underneath my Bloody Mary and tried to wipe away the smear. Wound up instead with paper bits and gummy paint between my fingers, just enough of a residue to linger, to distract.

And I bit my pickle, consciously reminding myself to move my jaw up and down, and wasted his confession, the one I thought I'd been waiting for all summer, thinking instead about dill pickles and the merits of turpentine and how on earth I hadn't noticed that errant streak of green earlier. All at a time when I would rather have stared like an infatuated teenager at the way the sun lit up his maple sugar hued hair.

Like reality or truth, I guess, the sun has this unflinching way about it. Too much make-up or bravado in the wrong light and you're busted. And there, in that bar all dark and red, the sun still found a way to creep through the Venetian slats and illuminate him with illusions of layers that when peeled back, seemed only to sting my shadowless eyes.

Across the table, my hands in his, he punctuated each point as though a politician. Continued to insist that I captured his interest, that I "GOT" him, that I'd won his love. And I thought, can love be won? And if I'd won, what the hell is it that I'd won? Why am I, alleged victor, sitting here a silent leftover, instead of prancing through the bar all smiles and victory waving flag in hand?

Maybe love is bigger than this. More pervasive, like the sun.

Was he thinking that, satisfied with my conquest, I could return to my empty bunk and fall asleep holding his white cable-knit sweater that smelled so much like campfire and like him. Be happy and eternally grateful for the rest of my life because, yes indeed, I won.

Anyway, I congratulated myself on winning his love. Scored imaginary points for my coup, pleased for the moment at the result of my willful ignorance. All the while still tripping on loving words I so desperately wanted to believe because such a sudden-death victory made me feel like I was worth something at last.

Another round of drinks arrived. He freed my hands but not the floor.

"I'm originally from the UK, you see, and needed a green card. She asked me to move in with her and after a couple of years, thought we ought to go through with the getting married part."

He didn't tell me he was going to leave her. I never really thought he would. Maybe that's not what I wanted. But maybe, just maybe, there was a tiny little part of me, oh let's say for argument's sake it was my heart, that thought I might be worth leaving for.

He started to speak in euphemism. Said we should "remember our time" as one might remember a lovely bouquet of flowers. Didn't say he'd remember licking my sticky, marshmallow-coated fingers, our secret late-night groping amongst the art supplies, our down and dirty sleeping-bag sex.

"The first time I saw you, I thought you were the most striking woman I had ever seen."

He was ruining everything with his talk.

Given the choices I had, I just wanted to kiss his forehead and tell him I loved him in a way I never thought I could love anyone. That I will continue to love him. Tell him that the time we had together was much longer than I ever loved any bouquet of flowers or lilac tree or any other cheese-ball comparison to what is fleeting and temporary. And that love is not external and does not come from him but from me, giving and giving till I bleed.

He continued.

Bloody hell.

"My son and daughter are the two most important things in my life, and you are right up there with them."

Could I ask for more: to be loved, even if at a distance, as unconditionally as a child?

"But, and I know this sounds kind of funny given the circumstances, I don't want to hurt my wife?"

Oh, I see. What she doesn't know won't hurt her. I could be forgiven the injury because through it all, I redeemed in him so much he thought he'd lost. Amazing how an impromptu blowjob will do that to a man who's been married for fifteen years.

So, I sat on my bar stool in the twenty-four-karat haze of the afternoon sun in Nowheresville, New York, blue sneakers dangling from the ends of my legs, pink sun-burned nose of a little kid, green paint stuck to my calf and now to my fingers, and supposed we were pretty lucky. We'd been able to have one last go, a chance to tidy up this messy affair lest its stain seep into autumn. Though I wished we'd left our talk of love back on the bedspread of the Ramada where it could, lost in time and peach flowers, remain forever ineffable and true.

"Even artists with wives, children and mortgages deserve to be happy and have real love," I reminded. I tried to persuade.

He listed the sacrifices he'd made to be with me, outlined the way of life he had risked. I didn't say anything then, just played with the straw in my drink and wondered. What would it be like to have your cake and eat it too? It wouldn't be hard to swallow, though it might leave decay in your conscience. There is such a thing as too much sugar.

So, I ended up consoling him, through vodka tomato sips like he was the one who would end up hurt in the end, as if I was the one with the dutiful wife awaiting my return. And he, the one who was never really mine to get away, kept talking out of his ass. I couldn't believe that this is how, by the shores of a finger lake as old and cold and glacial as carnal lust itself, I finally fell in love. Soon I'd be north again, entertaining myself with every man of the hour. Shaking my head at the sad, dark cliché I've become. Lying naked and spent on a polyester hotel bedspread, mourning my loss, his touch.

I ordered another bloody, bleeding-heart Mary and wondered how it was possible to feel so hollow and so full at the same time. Imagined him at home, wide-eyed and awake, thinking of me while she snuggled closer, and they called him Daddy.

FELICITY'S WORLD

Felicity's World

Okay. So, you gotta understand. Kevin and I had been going out for like three months. Three whole months and we never even did it once. Okay, well, technically we'd been fooling around. A lot. Let's just say we were getting close. Like I did some stuff to him and let him do some stuff to me, you know. So, we make this plan to do it, for real, last Friday night. We're there in the Charlie Cluck's Chicken and Ribs over on North Street South and he tells me this elaborate story so long and stupid and boring that I nearly finished my rabbit plate. I know, right? If I'd known what an asshole he was going to turn out to be I'd have ordered the mozza sticks *and* the Bourbon burger. So anyway, I'm sitting there across from him sipping my Diet Coke and he's not touching his French fries and it's driving me crazy like how bad I want one, but no way am I going to start filching stuff offa his plate and he's telling this long drawn-out story about skipping school that afternoon and going over to Rudy's house. You know, Rudy? The guy with the mole and the chin? He always wears that pink Ralph Lauren button down? So, I give him little smiles and nods like I'm listening. Offer up a laugh or two. Because Jason McFadden spilling beer on Rudy's dad's new pool table while they're watching hockey is just soooo funny. Not. Then we go to his house 'cause his whole family—mother, father, sister, brother—is out at this church thingy. They're like total Bible thumpers, by the way. Like, for real. Just wait! It gets better. So, we're fooling around on his couch and the next thing you know, I was sitting on his lap, straddled like, and kissing him and he carries me up to his bed. He reaches between the mattress and box spring, pulls out a roll of condoms. The purple kind. He holds them up and the roll just kind of flops into a string of like fifty. Like those lollipops they sell at Bargain Harold's around

Halloween with different colours all swirled together? So anyways we start laughing and then eventually get back to it and then, like, we did it. All the friggin' way. And it was so stupid. All that fuss for that? It hurt and it took like three seconds. Not even kidding. Three seconds. I was like, is that it? We're done? So anyhow, now it's official. I lost my V. Scratch that off the list.

But now I'm so mad. I found out something that is not very nice at all. It's just so stupid and unfair. Of course, I expected he'd tell his friends. And they'd be all like, hey dude, you took Felicity's virginity, way to go. Yeah: he *took* it. Maybe I *took* his, eh? What about that? No, it's all she's a slut and he's the man. Know what I mean? Double standard bullshit. And that's not even what I'm mad about! I mean that's just the stupid way it is. What really pissed me off was, okay, you know Glynis? She's my friend from volleyball, she goes to Bernard Memorial across town. She calls me up the "morning after." Saturday, super early, and tells me that she heard from her brother's best friend who goes to our school that all those guys weren't really at Rudy's house Friday afternoon. Oh no. They were at the Peacock Club ogling the strippers!

You know in books when someone gets crazy bad news and it says, she went white? That's what I felt like. Like someone pulled the bathmat out from under me and my head smashed on the side of the tub and I wound up with a split open head bleeding on the tile. I know, I know, it's not supposed to be a big deal, but it just made me so mad. Hurt, like that he would lie to me when we were about to do it. And I thought, you know? It's just like Mr. Garvey says: it's an equivocation. You know, like the witches in *Macbeth*. The telling of half-truths to mess up your head? Like, your parents tell you not to have one single person over when they are out and you have your whole class and then when they get back you say, no, I didn't have one single person over. So, it's misleading and lying. And if I'd known he was into that stripper shit I never would have done him. Not that my parents would ever leave me alone in the house. I don't know what they think I'm gonna do, burn the house down? Stick a forkful of spaghetti in the toaster? Sometimes it feels like they'd be happier if I was like that chick in the painting above the couch. Christina or whatever. She's this skinny, crippled looking thing in a pale-pink dress sitting in a big field looking at the house all peaceful and happy to be outside. That picture really bugs me. Okay, so they drive this girl in her wheelchair out into a field and dump it and then make her look at the house which is basically her prison 'cause she can't go anywhere on her own without her parents driving her and lifting her and shit. Maybe she wanted to look *away* from the house for a change, or whatever. But nope. Staring up at the big old farmhouse she can never leave. Depressing. Even old Helen Keller got up to stuff. Why would anyone want to hang *that* in their house? I know, right, *my* parents. That's like some kind of horror show. Her face should be all sulking and twisted, angry. Instead of so sweet and calm. I'd talk some sense into that Christina.

Ugh. I just can't believe I fell for Kevin. I'm so mad at myself. How could I be so stupid? The first night we hung out we were fooling around at, you know, that huge party over at Burp's place? Yeah, totally, that's the one. We were on his parents' bed, and I was talking about fate and star-crossed lovers, you know, like in *Romeo and Juliet*? Dumb drunk stuff, like, do you think our union has been foreordained? And Kevin was like, what, huh? Fate? That should have tipped me off that he had the IQ of a watermelon. Oh my God and you won't believe this. I was over at his place one night watching TV with him and his parents and this commercial for fuel, oil, maybe for Shell, comes on. It's these cave men banging on stuff with bones and wearing chunks of fur and then the music gets really loud and the camera cuts to a guy filling up a car at a gas station and a voice over goes, since the dawn of time... And Kevin's dad gets all mad and slaps his leg and shouts, where do they get this crap from! I'm thinking, uh duh, science? Kevin and I, we had this phone conversation one time about evolution, and he went right rangy. I'm not even kidding. He was talking all Adam's rib and the first people on earth and all that nonsense. Said evolution was just a theory and the evidence was in the Bible. And I was like, first of all, there's the big bang theory and second, there are rocks way older than any Bible bullshit and third, like duh? Dinosaurs? So stupid. His mom eventually got on the phone and told him to get off. I'm serious she did. Not because of what we were talking about. I think she was afraid he might knock me up me via the wires.

I can't believe he sat right across from me in Charlie Cluck's, in the haze of all things processed and modified, sucking the meat offa his buzzard wings and lying to my face. And then he goes and fucks me! And you know what else burns me? The fact that I thought it was me who was getting him all aroused. But no, he was getting a boner thinking about those stupid strippers jiggling their tits in his face. Can you even believe it? What kind of religion thinks it's more important to denounce dinosaurs than to respect women? I feel so bad for those women. Like half of them are forty and have kids and then having to go in and peel down for some rich Bible toting teenagers.

Whatever. I decided to get back at him. My mind was just spinning. Constantly scheming. How would I make him know how it feels to be made a fool out of by someone you actually had sex with for the very first time in your whole life! I wasn't going to be one of those stupid girls who half-slits her wrists or fake overdoses on a bottle of Tylenol for attention, leaving a goodbye cruel world note 'cause my boyfriend is so mean. No way. Of course, he'd be guilt ridden, devastated even. Except, one problem, I'd be, like, maimed or dead! Besides, with my luck I'd probably just barf all over myself and have to clean it up the next morning and my parents would find out and put me in counseling every Saturday night with a support group of lameos or some shit. So, then I thought maybe I should try starving myself, so I looked super skinny but, you know me, I have a hard enough time sticking to two shakes and a sensible dinner. So, I start thinking why should *I* be doing anything to *me* at all? He's the one who deserves to be punished. And my mind goes these crazy places, like, first, I'm thinking of all these ways I can get rid of him. Like kill him. But could I do it and not get caught? So, I pictured myself in army green fatigues and a beret like one of those vigilante Guardian Angels from New York City and I'm beating the crap out of him in a dark alley watching his head snap back off his neck each time I Kung Fu kick him. Or one of those Quebec biker-gang style drownings. I could lure him into some kind of sexual tie up game with coy looks and yellow rope. Stuff him into a sleeping bag with a couple of cinder blocks and plop, off a bridge. Except that a dead body in a bag full of cement would be way too heavy for me to lift. So, then I'd have to have help and the last thing I need is rats and stool pigeons leaking info to the fuzz.

You know? All Saturday I sat on my duvet, the one I hate that my mother forced me to get because it has sweet little pale brushstroke flowers on it. I wanted the bright one with black and red and blue and yellow graphics which is totally my style. Mom said it was "too loud." And that her choice was more "tasteful." Whatever. Anyway, I was lying there thinking: Kevin, how can I kill you, let me count the ways? Like, maybe I could take advantage of his shellfish allergy, take him to the Buoy O' Buoy Seafood and Spirits Emporium and slip a little shrimp into his orange roughy. At least I'd get to jab him with his epi-pen. Or maybe a drug overdose. I could make it look like an accident. It wouldn't even be that hard. Slip a little something extra into his drink at a party. A little acid, ecstasy, sleeping pills. Maybe a combo of all three. Maybe he'd choke on his own vomit. Poor Kevin. Who knew he had such a drug problem? Must be those strict Christian parents. Or maybe a push down some steep stairs. It worked for Tad on *The Winds of Lilac Hollow* when he needed to get rid of that ranch hand, Stone, in a big hurry. Or a fall from a teetering ladder hastily perched on the edge of his eavestrough. He'd gone over to help his girlfriend dig the leaves out when, Oops! Or a dive into some too shallow water egged on by his risk-taking girlfriend. Except spinals can be so tricky. I wouldn't want to have to stand around and wipe up his drool as he did his rehabilitation exercises and wheeled around all over the place in his electric wheelchair he controls with his mouth. And if I didn't, I'd look like a total bitch. Did he really think he was going to get away with it? Get away scot-free? That I wouldn't find out? Was that what he was hoping for? That I'd dump him so he wouldn't have to do the dirty work, he could just fuck me and go off with his friends laughing at me behind my back like I'm some dumb, dispensable, interchangeable hole?

It isn't fair. Guys can go see strippers, whack off to pictures of women with their legs all splayed, pussies wet and waiting. While I just fantasize about killing him, about getting even, and if I tell anyone, like, I mean, besides you, I'd probably have a team of psychiatrists breathing down my neck. Both perfectly natural acts of aggression if you ask me. If Kevin is a little more visual, maybe I'm a little more mental.

You know what bugs me? As soon as we break up, he is going to go off and do the same thing to another girl. He just gets to do whatever he wants. So. You wanna know what I did?

I called up his mom. And she was like, Oh Felicity. Shouldn't you be in school right now? And I go, I just couldn't bring myself to go today, Mrs. Mackenzie. I'm just so, sniffle sniffle, upset. I've been crying all morning. And she goes, what's the matter dear? And I'm like, it's really hard to talk about over the phone, like especially to Kevin's mother. But, but, I just thought you should know. (God she is such a bitch. You know what she told Kevin once? That they wanted him to have a girl-friend with a clearer Christian agenda. Yeah, seriously! And she suggests Debbie Arnold from their church. The one who changes in the bathroom into a pleather mini-skirt and all that black eyeliner as soon as her dad drops her off. It didn't take *her* three months to fuck *her* boyfriend. And Kevin never even told them I was great, or defended me, or anything. He said it was easier not to challenge them when they invoked religion. Imagine letting your parents control you like that? Never ques-tioning or thinking for yourself. No wonder he followed all those other dickheads to the Peacock Club.) Anyhow, his mom is like, you're not pregnant, are you? So I go, no, no, all in this sweet voice, but it has something to do with that. You see, it's Kevin and his friends. He's been hanging around these guys at school and they cut classes to go see the strippers at the Peacock Club. And last Friday, while you guys were out at church he was pressuring me to have… to fornicate with him. He keeps all these condoms under his mattress. I don't know how many times he's done it before or whatever. And…, I go, he's telling everyone at school that I'm a goodie goodie and that God wouldn't have given us private parts if he didn't want us to use them. I'm scared Mrs. Mackenzie. I don't want to lose Kevin, I love him ever so much. But I want to save my virginity for my husband on our wedding night. I totally did say that too. She's all like, you just stick to your guns, and protect your virginity and all this garbage. It's because of the Peacock Club, I tell her. And she's like, Peacock Club? And I'm like, the place with the dancers who take off their clothes out by the provincial park? And she goes, but they're underage. Some of them have fake IDs, I say. And she tells me not to worry, she'll take care of things, so I hang up the phone and start laughing. Rolling around on my flowered duvet just laughing.

So last week, I decide I need to plant some evidence. I go over to the Peacock Club at lunch break, borrowed my dad's car. That's right, middle of the day all by myself. Felicity Carmichael struttin' on up to the Peacock Club. I walked right inside. It was dark and dirty, like everything had a layer of jizz on it. There were lights over a stage, and I could see a woman slinking around but she still had her bra and unders on. She had, like, kind of a fat stomach. And there were two guys in big caps, you know, the kind with the mesh backs? Yeah, they were eating hamburgers and drinking beer. Gross, eh? I kept thinking: Can we get you something to eat with your erection? Eww. Pathetic, really, and not sexy at all. It wasn't how I imagined. I grabbed a book of fancy matches from off the bar, black with a gold and turquoise peacock feather, and pulled over in Martin's field by the seventh concession to smoke half an old joint. You know what it says in gold scrip on the back of the matches? The Peacock Club: Where men come to play. With themselves! That's what I said too! Anyhow, after school, I meet up with Kevin and give him a big hug, tell him all is forgiven and then slip the roach into his back pocket and the matches in the centre console of his mom's Tempo. Guy like that? Guaranteed his mom still does his laundry. But that isn't even the best part!

Did you see the paper today? NEWLIFE BIBLE CHAPEL PICKETS PEACOCK CLUB. Kevin's mom is on the front page with a crowd in front of the Peacock Club holding up all these churchy signs! Stuff like: "Say it isn't Sodom and Gomorrah. And East of Toronto, Not East of Eden." They quoted her in the paper and everything. Now—get this—they are circulating a petition for the club's closure.

Can you even believe it? Well, I think calling me a genius is a little strong. Okay. Powerful, maybe, I'd agree with that.

the present the present the present the present the present
the present the present the present the present the present the
present the present the present the present the present the present
the present the present the present the present the present the
present the present the present the present the present the
present the present the present the present the present the present
the present the present the present the present
the present the present the present
the present the present the present the
present the present the present
the present the present the pre
ent the present the present the
present the present the pre
ent the present the present
the present the present the
present the present the pre
sent the present the present
the present the present the
present the present the
present the present the
the present the present the
the present the present the
present the present the
present the present the
present the present the
present the present the pre
ent the present the present
the present the present th
the present the present the
present the present the pre
the present the present th
present the present the pre
the present the present
the present the present
the present the present
the present the present
the present the present
the present the present th
present the present the
present the present the
present the present the
present the present
the present the present
the present the present
the present the present
the present the present
the present the present
the present the present

THE PRESENT
THE PRESENT
THE PRESENT
THE PRESENT
THE PRE
SENT THE PR
THE PRESENT
THE PRE
THE P
RE
P

THE PRESENT THE PRE
THE PRE SENT
THE PRESENT

THE PRESENT THE PAS
THE PR
THE PRESENT THE

THE PRESENT
THE PRE

THE PRESEN
THE PRE

THE PRESENT THE PRESENT
PRESENT THE PRESENT
THE PRESENT THE
PRESENT THE
THE PRESENT THE
PRESENT THE
THE

The Present

Hugo held up his hand, fingers spread. "Five minutes. Cab'll be here in five minutes," he whispered to Holly, "C'mon. Let's go," not wanting to wake his in-laws or the kids, all of whom were sleeping upstairs. Holly stood at the kitchen counter digging through her purse taking inventory: cellphone, charger, Chapstick, wallet, passports, emergency tampons, headphones, spare underpants, hand sanitizer, sunglasses, Kleenex, Imodium, *The Portable Dorothy Parker*, everything she could need while in transit for their trip to Jamaica.

They stood bundled in their winter coats in the front hall anticipating the cab's approach. Each looked out a glass side panel flanking the door and onto the early morning mist glowing amber from the still lit streetlight. Hugo flipped the porch switch. Red floodlights beamed mercilessly into their eyes. It was almost as if a spaceship had landed on their small, snow-covered front lawn, two foreign red orbs intentionally blinding earth's inhabitants. Holly clenched her teeth, shielded her eyes from the onslaught.

"So," said Hugo, "you like what I did with the Christmas lights?"

"Sure," said Holly. Silence followed as each cast awkward glances up, down, at each other, anywhere but head on into the glare. Then Holly, tongue tense with restraint said, "I'm sorry. I appreciate the time and effort you took it's just that usually with floodlights they're set back from the house to illuminate the house as a whole with like a rising cascade of crimson rather than searing the retinas of onlookers."

"Whatever," said Hugo, huffing a laugh. "You do it next year."

Holly smiled. Whatever was right. What did it matter that their boxy, white St. John's house with the inset vestibule of a porch glowed red rendering it rather mouth-like, it was, she supposed, in its own cavernous way, festive. They were off to Jamaica. Relaxation! Renewal! Reconnection! And it was right too that next year she probably would wind up doing the lights as well. She'd just add it to the list.

The week before Christmas was a crummy time to go on vacation. Holly, a teacher, had school holidays, and her parents, the babysitters, always wintered in Portugal shortly after Christmas, and summered at the cabin, so were only available within a certain window. The timeframe on the trip for Hugo and Holly had been quickly closing as well. They needed to go before February in order to use the voucher they'd won in a Rotary raffle at last year's Valentine's Day Gala for seven rejuvenating days at an all-inclusive, exclusive, couples resort. And it couldn't come soon enough, thought Holly. Their biggest couple's outing since their youngest daughter was born two and a half years ago was last winter—trivia night at the Grumpy Stump. She recalled that being the last time they'd had sex with each other as well. How many months ago was that? Had it been a year? The cab whisked them away to the airport. Holly felt the red Christmas lights throbbing in her periphery.

On the plane, a man slept in the aisle seat of their assigned trio. Hugo gallantly allowed Holly the window side for which she was most grateful. She looked out the oval. It had just started snowing St. John's kind of snow: heavy, wet, translucent flakes you couldn't do anything with but wait for the rain to come and wash them all away clearing the slate for the next miserable deluge.

With winter coats stowed in their suitcases before boarding, the plane seemed cold. Holly reached above and turned the little air dial off, then did the same for Hugo as he'd already fallen asleep. She took the small book out of her purse and read a few of the shortest stories, clicked the light off, did the buttons up on her denim jacket and looked over at Hugo's light fleece enviously. As if he could sense her neediness by osmosis, he wrapped the coat a little tighter around himself tucking the edges in and snoring in a discreet, irregular pattern. In the glow of the non-smoking light above their heads Holly examined the way his face slumped over the shoulder closest to her, the wrinkles and stubble packed creases between his chin and neck. I hate him, she thought. She didn't mean to think such a thing, she didn't even really believe it herself, but there it was swaying like stained underpants in the backyard of her mind.

Holly took her compact out of her purse and looked at her own aging face. When she'd had her hair highlighted blonde last week, she'd had the most curious conversation with the shampoo girl. The girl, a young woman, was a biology student at Memorial University specializing in entomology and working in the salon part-time. Holly had asked her quite specifically what she'd been studying: polyandry and nuptial gifts in insects. Holly had made a joke about crabs and mate selection, that for female crabs, it wasn't just the size of his claws, but how he waved them from across the beach. The shampoo-girl-come-entomologist laughed and went on to explain that some nuptial gifts were nutritious and edible, a dead bug perhaps, meant for consumption during or after copulation to enhance the female's fecundity and the health of her offspring. In the case of the field cricket, she said, the bigger the gift, the more the investment for the male, consequently, the more likely he'd be involved with paternal activity. While a male beetle with a smaller offering, makes less of an investment and as a result has more to spread around between other females. Seminal gifts could be proffered by many different males, accepted, and stored by certain female ants and spiders who would then have a genetic mixed bag of babies depending on who, and how many "gifts" the mother accepted. Though, she went on, such polyamorousness could result in sexual conflict as the male insect in these cases minimally participated in offspring rearing. In other words, when female insects had choice and power, they rarely submitted to, or relied on, a single male, unless he had a lot to offer. Holly would miss her when she'd graduated and gotten herself a job in the field instead of the salon. She plugged in her headphones and scrolled through the movie listings on the seat back in front of her finally choosing *White Christmas*. How on earth would Bing Crosby and Danny Kaye manage to croon and soft shoe their way out of this one?

In Toronto, they boarded a second plane. While Hugo slept, Holly flipped through the pages of the inflight magazine, stared at a photo of an old cigar-smoking woman from Havana, and read the accompanying article on cigar making in Cuba. On the back page a banking ad showed in black and white, a couple sitting under an ornate light post in Venice. The man, looking gently off into the distance, had an arm draped over the woman's shoulder; the woman, gazing up at him, had her arms around his waist. The way she was looking at him, Holly's not sure she has ever looked at anyone that way.

The airport shuttle bumped along the road to the resort passing tin-sided huts and spitting the two of them out onto a stone path lined with gardens heaping with begonias, hibiscus, assorted other blossoms and the scent of frangipani. Mr. Roarke and Tattoo, or their modern Jamaican counterparts, scurried Hugo and Holly's luggage away between Doric columns and trays of pink champagne.

In their room, on the pillows of their plump, white king bed, were peach hibiscus blossoms and a single towel swan. "Well," said Holly, "here we are."

"Yes," agreed Hugo jumping in between the two blooms and crossing his ankles, "here we are." Holly walked to the window where the ocean in the distance lapped the shore, two blue swimming pools sparkled in the sunlight and the dark silhouette of a palm tree on the side of a pink building imprinted itself in her memory. "Should we…" Hugo grabbed the swan by the throat. "Or do you want to get something to eat?"

The smell of jerk chicken hung in the air. Holly was starving. She also wanted to have a nice holiday without any sulking or arguing of any sort and she was pretty sure there was only one way to make that happen. She advanced to the bed and performed fellatio after which Hugo nearly fell asleep. Holly complained. He dragged himself off the bed.

Everywhere, well-fed white people held hands and strolled. Marriage ceremonies took place under white lattice arbors. Photographers snapped pictures of embracing couples in front of the setting sun. Lovers, gently pickled, marinated further in briny hot tubs canoodling and smooching sloppily. Tennis balls thumped between agreeable partners, words like forty and love bouncing through the air and taking on new meaning. White marble fountains of reared up horses spat and dribbled water out of equine mouths. A peacock trotted across the giant black and white chessboard where Hugo and Holly played, and, as if proposing a challenge of its own, flashed its plumage. Everything around them conspired romance. But their mojitos had been sweet, their jerk chicken insipid, the coral reef they'd snorkeled, bleached out and bland, save for a few dark purple anemones and a small school of pale-yellow fish and Holly struggled to find things to say to Hugo, feeling at times like her mother who tended to fill silences with banal observations: *Look at the darling vestibule draped with bougainvillea! There's Neptune's Lounge. That might be nice for dinner.* And Hugo had yet to reach for her hand or gaze longingly into her eyes.

Mornings, the sand was littered with people browning and sizzling themselves like so many strips of bacon, yellow and white striped umbrellas, books, and fluffy white towels splayed out around them. The men reading such and such by Tom Clancy, the titles indiscernible compared to the author's name; the women reading *Fifty Shades of Grey,* its book jacket of swirling silver tie undone, the author's name ambiguous. Hugo and Holly ate and swam and soaked and swilled and waterskied, the latter activity leading to the securing of a small bag of Jamaica's finest from the boat driver. At one of the resort gift shops they bought T shirts, hats, and a sand globe for the kids as well as an expensive package of rolling papers eventually walking as far as they could away from the resort in all its myriad shades of forced romance and along the white sand beach. Hugo rolled them a joint on the flat of his stomach. They sat together in the warm sand burying their feet and smoking, looking out into the Caribbean Sea the colour of Colgate Gel. Waves curled ashore, hesitating and then retreating pulling a little sand back out with each ethereal beckon. Holly dove her hands into the sand marveling at its warmth, the sensation of tiny grains rolling around and through her fingers, getting stuck under the sapphire on her left hand. She reached for Hugo's thigh. He didn't pull away nor did he put his hand on hers.

"Why her?" she asked. "She wasn't even pretty." She glanced at his face; he stared up at the clouds through his new Maui Jim's.

"Proximity," he said. "Why him?"

"Attention, affection, I guess." Holly examined her long pink and white legs stretched out toward the shore like raw, unfurled shrimp. Then they both lay back in the hot sand listening to the waves until the light of the sun pixelated into orange and then faint yellow and finally into pink.

The next evening at an outdoor BBQ festival with a live reggae band, their room number was drawn out of a hat. A woman from the resort announced they'd won a private dinner for two on the beach with butler service. In the dark of the beach at dusk, sat a white hut with a table, candle lit and strewn with rose petals, a bottle of champagne chilling in a silver bucket beside a white gloved butler four feet from their tent. Holly kicked her sandals off under the table crunching the cold damp sand with her toes. They spoke briefly of home, the kids, work; they wondered together how the grandparents were getting along. When the champagne was gone and a bottle of red poured, Hugo reminisced about the last time he'd come to Jamaica with a girlfriend in his youth, how much fun they'd had riding scooters and smoking pot. Having heard the story previously, Holly nodded politely.

Back in their room, she stood at the end of the bed and steeling herself, embraced Hugo. And they tried to kiss, but it was as forced and awkward as the dinner. They flopped on their backs in the beautifully made-up bed squashing the fresh towel swan beneath them. "Where does it go?" she wondered aloud.

"Huh?" said Hugo.

"Where does love go when it dies," she said.

Hugo said nothing for a moment and then, "maybe it's like fat. You know when people lose a lot of fat it sort of evaporates and get breathed out into the air."

"Yeah," said Holly, "maybe."

And seemingly, just as soon as they had arrived, it was time to bid farewell to the tropical heat, the palm tree silhouettes, the charcoal and spice scented air, their suitcases packed again and lined up for loading onto the shuttle, their room vacant, awaiting the next round of hopeful fools.

Snow flanked the outer ring road. Great globs of it splattered onto the windshield of an orange cab which subsequently deposited them neatly back into St. John's, back to the cold salt air, back to their glowing red door and straight into the gaping jaws of Christmas.

One
Man's
Garbage

One Man's Garbage

"Should I put *this* out?" he asked on the Friday night before the sale. *This* was a handmade pottery bowl. "I think it was a wedding gift, but I have no particular attachment to it." He handed it over for her perusal.

Sally examined the bowl, her brow furrowed. The pottery was thin, the colour muted sage, the surface matte except for a layer of black-glazed floral drizzles and wasn't quite round. The imperfection of a thin wobbled edge seemed to excuse the bowl from the banality of pasta salad or tortilla chips. The potter's inference of flaw set it apart from other serving dishes, made it art, a *piece* to be displayed and commented upon.

My what a lovely bowl.

Thank you, it was the first in our collection, she might add if indeed that had been the truth.

Not to worry, Sally wasn't gauche enough to sully such a delicate piece with mounds of gloopy, flatulent bean dip. Douglas might not think she knows much, but she knows *that* much. She loved the bowl's quality, its beauty, wished it were she who had received it as a wedding gift. Even if she ever had married, it was not the sort of present her friends and family would've chosen. She'd have received steak knives, magazine racks, and potholders, maybe a set of bathroom towels, a Pyrex mixing bowl or a bed in a bag from Sears. Of course, there would be no wedding.

"Let's keep it," she said, looking casually at Douglas, hoping not to perceive signs of nostalgia. "It's beautiful."

"Guess it is kinda nice," he said and put it back on the middle glass shelf of the wall unit. He looked around the rest of the living room with worn-out blue eyes and gestured like a salesman in a showroom, as if to suggest perfunctorily that she had carte blanche. "So, what else do you think we should get rid of, Sall?"

"Well," Sally paused, pretending to look about the room as if she had never considered such a possibility. As if she hadn't fantasized a hundred, a thousand times about using her forearm to bulldoze all the framed pictures of Teddy, Douglas's four-year dead cocker spaniel, off of the back of the upright piano, from the mantel, from the top of the stereo. From every conceivable surface where a framed picture of a dead dog could be.

She spoke softly, as if to cushion the blow. "How about some of these picture frames? I mean, how many pictures of Teddy do we really need around the house? You know, new chapter and all?" She touched his brawny shoulder and gave a look she hoped conveyed tenderness.

Douglas looked around, took in the evidence. "Okay," he said, his voice that of a man beaten down by compromise, a man tired of living alone. "Just leave a few and the rest can go out." He scratched the back of his newly shorn hair with newly cropped nails. Sally thought she saw more grey than she had just six weeks ago. He passed her the cardboard box and left the room, attending, presumably, to tasks of more significance.

She'd anticipated a disagreement, perhaps even a fight. A conversation at least. Since when had Douglas become so flexible, so accommodating? Not long ago she'd rearranged his—their—kitchen cupboards more efficiently, sure he'd be dazzled by her organizational prowess. Proudly she stood, cupboard doors open, hands raised "Ta Da!" Tupperware lids on one side, containers on the other, glasses near the sink, plates above the stove. Douglas practically dug his heels into the linoleum so he could better snort and hoof at Sally all the reasons why everything in *his* kitchen, in *his* house, in *his* life, had to stay exactly the same. That *Caroline* always had everything *her* way in the kitchen and now that *he* had *his* own place *he* was going to do things *his* way. Next day, the kitchen was back to his preferred order.

So now, *this*. This sudden agreeability over picture frames. It was enough to give her hope. And while Sally knew that hopeful feelings unrealized could quickly turn to resentment, she couldn't help herself: the tingle of forever after crept giddily up her spine. But, wait. She'd been ripped-off. She deserved that fight. She needed to say, "Wait just a bloody minute, Doug, I will not be responsible for cleaning out your emotional closet. Here's the box, you do it."

On the other hand, there was this gilt-framed picture of Caroline with Teddy that Sally would be more than happy to smash with a brick, have at the metal frame with her tin snips, then rip the photo into pieces and flush them down the crapper. If only it could be that easy. The photograph sat on top of the television so that every time Sally watched one of her programs, all she could see, all she could think of, was Douglas, Caroline, and Teddy. It wasn't the picture so much as its place of prominence, like she could never forget for a second the importance of what and who had come before. Maybe it was the picture too. Skinny Caroline with her blond bob, small upper lip mole and white teeth grinning out at all the bullshit Sally was having to sort through.

After months of Douglas's urging, after Sally finally agreed to move in, she was shocked he'd left the picture up and on the TV. He swore up and down and on his still living mother's grave that he wanted to start fresh, wanted the proverbial clean slate. Sally couldn't believe he was going to force her, by his own avoidance, to point it out and beg him to take it down. She shouldn't have to ask, damn it. There's more to joining two lives together than just emptying a few sock drawers and pushing aside suits in the closet to make way for Sally's dresses. Didn't Douglas know that? How could he not know *that*? As if all her bras, underwear and hosiery would even fit in those emptied out bureau drawers. She'd had to set up additional storage in a portable Rubber Maid unit in the closet. Ah well. No point dwelling on it now. She had no intention of spending the rest of her days with Douglas squabbling over trivial things.

If only she could be certain that these picture-related incidents were harmless oversights, weird bachelorisms—like his pantry full of baked beans and Rice-a-Roni—and not perpetual unrequited longing. He denied still loving her. He told Sally *she* was the only one for him now. She'd tried to believe him, but the picture. That damn picture.

He, their relationship, had so much potential, so much promise. She'd best take advantage of the opportunities that came her way and discreetly dispose of the photos without fuss. Leave it to Sally to put her head down and do the dirty work. Growing up, she was the one who looked after her little sister, she was the one who did the dishes every night, the one who emptied the cat litter. In college, she was the roommate scrubbing vomit off the bathroom floor the day after the big party while everyone else slept. Faithful, dependable, always to be counted on Sally, every day plunging her face into her patients' open jaws to polish, floss, and fluoride mouths for dental inspection.

She carried the cardboard box to the piano and considered which picture frames to set out for public sale and which to keep. She hardly cared anymore. Teddy on surfboard with sunglasses, into the box. Teddy with Canadian flag cape at Parliament Hill, into the box. Teddy asleep in the hallway, Teddy in a pile of raked leaves, Teddy dressed as a Halloween bumblebee, Teddy and Santa, Teddy swimming, Teddy with a bandana, Teddy in black tie, Teddy and Caroline, into the box. Sometimes Sally wished she could garner half as much adulation and affection as that damn dead dog. Where were the pictures of Sally? Still, if Douglas could love that deeply, the way he seemed to love Teddy, when—and if—they had a child, he'd be capable of great, selfless love. She loved him for who she knew he could be.

As Sally carried the box to the garage and plunked it down on one of the card tables laden with stuff, she sighed and clucked her tongue. So, she'd never be thin and beautiful walking on her father's arm down the aisle in a white wedding dress to a handsome young man who had never loved anyone like he loved her.

Who did she think she was? Cinderfuckinella? Gorgeous, slim-footed and elegant she was not. At least she had someone. She could be old and single, whiling her evenings away watching previously recorded episodes of *General Hospital*, cramming cookies into her gob one after the other, growing fatter and fatter by the second, fantasizing about Doctor Money Bags, chief of surgery, sweeping her away to his private paradise. That would definitely be worse.

She sorted through some of the items Douglas had meticulously spaced for customer inspection on the makeshift tables and plywood-topped sawhorses. He'd set up the tables in a U shape around the garage and planned to place larger items on the lawn to entice passersby, weather permitting. Rain or shine the sale would go on. He was practical that way.

All the tchotchkes she'd carted around with her over the years lay in wait, cheapened by masking tape, and felt pen prices. Why had she lugged this stuff so many places? No matter who she'd lived with, a gaggle of roommates or any one of several irresponsible boyfriends, somehow having that papier mache egg in the brass holder or the batik fish wall hanging or the mauve and lime green chenille afghan she'd knit had always made it feel like home. They were her things, things she'd made or chosen. Real originals. Part of her wanted to collect them and put them around his house. Their house, her house too. It wasn't like she needed them now. Did she?

Douglas was fifteen years older than Sally. At a Community Centre Halloween dance, she'd been disguised as Princess Leia, and Douglas, a toasted western, not that she could tell that immediately from his costume. He'd dressed as a cowboy then hung pieces of toast from his Stetson with string. She bumped into him in a queue at the beer tent and before she could apologize, a patient from the dental clinic dressed as Darth Vader slapped her on the back and slurred wet words into her ear. As she turned to the poor cowboy she'd hit, she noticed a piece of toast had wedged itself between one of her braided wig buns and ripped.

"Does this belong to you?" she said.

He looked at her broken offering. "Shit. My toast."

Sally learned quickly that Douglas had already done the big wedding-divorce thing and wasn't eager to repeat the exercise. She'd seen the pictures, six ushers, six bridesmaids, a real expensive affair. And she'd heard all about fabulous Caroline and her passion for golf, her love of fine wine and aged steaks. Sally sometimes wondered what Douglas saw in her plain old white bread self. What would he say about her? That she liked silly puns, mystery novels and raunchy late-night conversations with old friends from high school? Charmed, I'm sure. That she kept a box of Kleenex beside her while she watched the Sunday night disease-of-the-week movie? How sophisticated. That Kraft Dinner doused in ketchup was one of her culinary favourites? What a connoisseur.

He'd tease Sally, saying she was built for comfort, but he was no centerfold himself. And Sally could sure do with a little more romance, a little more passion. A sensual massage, a bottle of champagne, candles, a trail of rose petals leading toward the bed, flowers with stems even, chocolate. Hell, anything resembling an effort would suffice.

Sometimes, when she'd had enough of the suitcases behind Douglas's eyes and of the regurgitated fluoride from the mouths of strangers, she would sneak home for lunch to have the run of the place. Would spill drips on the counter and refuse to wipe them until after she'd eaten. Would stare, without forethought, into the fridge. Had Douglas been home, he'd have followed her around complaining and wiping and crumb catching with his multi-coloured Pier One dishrag. She'd blast the Sex Pistols or the Clash so loud the pictures on top of the stereo cabinet would rattle reminding her of the time, not that long ago, when she wore ripped fish nets, black lace-up boots and never gave a thought to her future. Especially not to sustaining some less than perfect relationship. And with music blaring, she'd scream along, *"Should I stay or should I go now, if I stay there will be trouble, if I go it will be double, so c'mon, baby, let me know, should I stay or should I go?"*

She scrutinized the tables in the garage. There was the cobalt blue and white lamp she'd made in a pre-Douglas ceramics class. She'd asked his permission to bring it out from basement storage, to tuck it in the corner of a room somewhere; she knew it wasn't beautiful, but it reminded her of the class and of the friends she'd made and it made her smile. Douglas, halfway out the door on his way to play golf, said: *I'd rather not have it out, Sall. It's not to my taste.* She sulked for a couple of days but hadn't given up. She stroked the back of his neck as he liked and asked if they could use her purple and cream checked duvet cover instead of his plain navy bedding. He shook his head, wrinkled up his nose as if she'd asked him to replace it with the cat box and said: *It doesn't go with my décor.*

She scanned the garage. It smelled of gas and motor oil. Most of the rejected stuff, it seemed, was hers. Douglas had promised to get rid of some things as well. A dim pendulum of a bulb cast a haze over a few pieces of old sports equipment around the perimeter. Skates, skis, tennis rackets. Not just old and out of fashion but stuff he couldn't even use anymore since his knee operation two winters ago. Yet, there in the cobwebbed corner was the table Sally had refinished. Burned delicate tendrils of ivy into each corner with a special crafty tool, added a slight wash of green to some of the leaves and a few coats of matte polyurethane. There had to be a space somewhere in this big house for her little table. In her apartment it was one of the first thing guests, friends had noticed. *Oh Sally, they'd say, you're so creative.*

Sally turned away from the loss and went inside. Maybe Douglas would be there to share a drink. Maybe she'd cover his neck, his ears with gentle kisses. Plead the case of the unneeded table. But Douglas was in bed. She poured herself a stiff Drambuie and sat in front of the blank television, staring at the space where Caroline's picture used to be.

Well, Sally thought, if I'm ever going to feel at home in this sterile museum, I'm going to have to get off my butt and take action. Full of gumption and Drambuie, she stomped to the garage, retrieved her lamp and peeled the price sticker off. There. She finished her drink and watched the tail end of a rerun police drama, then, careful not to wake Douglas, slipped into bed.

Next morning they awoke early for a Saturday, finished pricing their junk and set items out on the lawn for the sale. They hadn't been out of the house fifteen minutes when early birds began to scavenge. Pick-up trucks and mini vans, rusted out economy cars and luxury sedans descended on the street in front of their house, desperate to grab a cut-rate piece of them. An old woman with fine white hair poking out from underneath a kerchief and an osteo hump on her back the size of an overturned wok, held up Sally's batik fish.

"How much ya want for this?" she asked Douglas gruffly. She had a shifty gaze that suggested she would not be swindled out of one red cent.

Douglas scanned the yard for Sally. Assuming he was in the clear, he seized the moment. "I'll tell you what," he said, "I'll give *you* a dollar if you take it off my hands."

The woman grinned, eyes disappearing into wrinkled, cavernous sockets as she stuffed the fish into her red-striped tote. She elbowed Douglas, unzipped a small coin purse and motioned for him to deposit the dollar.

Sally, who'd witnessed the whole thing from across the lawn, felt hurt rise up her chest, blood throb in her ears. A couple, not much younger than she, waved at her from the driveway: What was the price of the Autumn Spice Corning Ware fondue pot? They dropped three bucks into the pocket of the apron Douglas had bought for the occasion. Sally gave away her green kitchen canisters for a few dollars, her Japanese tea set for fifteen, her table for twenty-five. Watched helplessly, mute and paralyzed, as strangers fingered and poked and judged and bought her old life for a pittance.

The garage full of people, Douglas hugged her. "We're doing great, honey." So, this is what it felt like to be nickeled and dimed to death. Worst of all, she was letting him.

By eleven thirty, the lawn had been picked down to its bones. Sally went inside. Lay down on top of the duvet, careful not to disrupt Douglas's throw cushions. Could hear him humming, light of foot and heart. He shouted up the stairs for Sally to save up her appetite that they'd go out for a nice steak dinner tonight on the proceeds. Sally said nothing, rolled over and hugged her borrowed pillow.

When they returned from the restaurant, glutted with wine and beef, they plopped down onto the sofa to watch television. On the table beside the TV, to the left of her lamp, sat the picture of Caroline and Teddy. Sally stood up, adjusted her sagging panty hose and pointed at the photo. And in the still light of the den, said, "I'm not looking at this friggin' picture of your ex-wife every single day of my life! Get rid of it, Douglas, or I'm leaving!" She hadn't meant for it to come to this, she hadn't wanted to overreact, she didn't really care about the picture *that much*. She had never wanted to be so petty.

Douglas grabbed the framed photo, threw it into the drawer of the console and shut it with a terminal slam. The glass shattered as the frame hit the back of the drawer.

It's still there, Douglas, she thought. It's still there.

INSIDE PASSAGES

Inside Passages

She buckled the five-point restraint system over her daughter's small chest, tightened and double-checked the straps. Even though Alicia was now four, Elizabeth ignored her pleadings for a booster seat, and kept her in the middle of the back hoping it might be safer somehow if the unthinkable happened. Now she'd be driving halfway around Georgian Bay, Collingwood to Penetanguishene, almost an hour each way, every day. It was okay now, in September, but in a couple of months when the wind ripped across that vast expanse of water and the snow blew from shore to farmer's fields across the highway, she'd be totally fucked. She reminded herself not to worry about things she could not control, that the future is unpredictable. She reminded herself to embrace the commute, to use the time to talk and sing with Alicia, to turn this potential negative into a positive.

Six forty-five a.m. Alicia's head slumped over to her shoulder, pale eyelids shut, mouth agape. Elizabeth had been going on pure adrenalin since Dan left a month ago. She was lucky to have this job. It was a gift. She sipped hot coffee from a travel mug and nibbled the crumbling edge of a granola bar as she drove. The CBC Ontario morning hosts chattered quietly in the background. Alicia's breakfast—a sliced apple, some cheese, and part of a bran muffin—sat untouched in Tupperware on the passenger seat.

She flexed her fingers around the curve of the steering wheel. Foolishly, she had put her faith in the wrong person, put her faith in Dan instead of in herself. That was the problem: not trusting herself, not trusting her instincts. *Embrace the gift*, she whispered softly under her breath. *Embrace the gift.*

Penetanguishene: Ojibwa for *land of white rolling sands*. First settled by the Huron, followed by Étienne Brûlé and the Jesuits in the 1600s, home to the British during the War of 1812, then to displaced Québécois and Métis afterwards, and now land of maximum-security mental institutions for the criminally insane and Canada's first Super Jail. It was the nation's first prison for profit, a recently procured contract between a private American corporation (HRTC, based in Houston, Texas), and the newly elected, ultra-conservative provincial government. New Premier Mike Harris wanted to make a point of trimming government fat, of bullying through his "commonsense revolution." Could prisons be run better and cheaper by private companies than by the province? Harris and his ilk believed so. The one common-sense thing Elizabeth understood was that you don't make a man better by locking him in a cage and treating him like shit. Maybe she could do some good with this job.

Elizabeth tried to be optimistic about her role, to be right-minded in her intentions. Her work here was hardly altruistic, though; the business of punishment paid well. She was slated for a full-time schedule, teaching four ninety-minute periods per day: two English, one Parenting, and one Introduction to Computers. The computer course scared her a bit since she had only rudimentary knowledge and zero interest in the subject, but the vice-principal had assured her it was really just the basics. Maybe he was just desperate to fill the job. The English class she was expected to teach on PC scared her most of all. PC—Protective Custody, where all the sexual offenders were housed lest the GP, General Population, figured out who did what to whom and beat the crap out of them. Or worse.

The granola bar flip-flopped in a swirl of coffee, and a knob of apprehension wormed its way up her chest getting stuck some-where between her heart and her throat. She'd read the insider's manual, read about how inmates groom staff for favours, coaxing them into being mules for tobacco and other contraband. She was going to have to be strong. She was going to have to really say no and mean it; she was going to have to learn to assert herself—for once. She'd been to the jail a couple of times for training and orientation, but this would be her first day in the classroom. If you could call Multi-purpose Room Three a classroom: cream brick walls, Plexiglas windows, a blue panic button on the wall. God—would she have to press it?

It was also Alicia's first day at her new daycare. Elizabeth had selected it because it was run by the Y, same as the morning pre-school she'd attended last year. She hoped this would give Alicia a sense of continuity and it was close to the jail. As she neared Penetang, Elizabeth inserted a Barney CD and cranked the volume, then reached back with her right hand and jiggled Alicia's leg. She tried to get her to open her juice box and take a few bites of cheese.

"I'm so tired, Mommy. Why do we have to get up so early?"

"It's just what we have to do right now."

As Elizabeth pulled into the nearly empty parking lot of the childcare center, she fished around the glove box for the bag of wipes to clean her daughter's sticky hands. Conscious of the tight timeline—she needed to leave enough time to get through all the security checks before organizing for class—she rushed little Alicia, who dragged her legs and her Barbie knapsack all the way up to the door. She was a good kid. Hung her belongings up in the cubby, smiled at the new staff, kissed and hugged her mom good-bye.

On approach, the prison looked like a movie set. Tall fence tops with curled snarls of razor wire. Grey-brick and metal interrupting the roadside rhythm of old-growth spruce. She'd seen the aerial photographs: six interconnected octagonal pods surrounded by forest. Each pod had six living units with a hundred and ninety-two beds. She would teach on units four, five and six. Elizabeth parked the Escort, patted its dashboard in a show of gratitude for the safe drive, and then laughed at herself. Her little superstitions weren't going to help her now. As she walked to the front doors, she tilted her head up, noted the security cameras, and thought about the institution for the criminally insane just a little way down the street overlooking the bay. It could be worse. She could be over there teaching parenting to Hannibal Lecter. She took her last full, deep breath of genuine fresh air for the day and opened the door.

Vanessa, whom Elizabeth had met during orientation, was waiting for her at Checkpoint Charlie, the first security desk where all staff signed in and picked up their Man Down Units. The correctional officer told Elizabeth to be sure she checked that the unit was in working order as she passed by central control on the way to the teachers' offices on unit six.

"So, are you nervous?"

"A little."

"Don't be. I've been teaching here since it opened in the spring. Nothing's ever happened. Well, I guess I shouldn't say that. Nothing major. You'll see. Honestly, I think the COs are worse to deal with than the inmates."

"Why?"

"Couple of reasons. First, they don't like us or the social workers because they think we're too soft on the inmates. Call us 'con huggers.' And then there's all this union shit going down because of the privatization. They're pretty pissed about that. Can't say as I blame them. Imagine if some U.S. company got a contract with the government to run the school board and then wouldn't allow any unionized teachers to work there? Brutal. Still, doesn't excuse them being assholes."

They stood in front of the next security door, waiting for the CO to buzz them through into a small room with a second CO. They put their lunches, briefcases, and purses on a conveyor belt that moved them through an x-ray machine like airport security. Then each walked through a metal detector. Elizabeth wondered if it was healthy to be subjecting her food and body to this process every day. The CO buzzed them through.

Vanessa glanced at her watch. "You might want to get here a bit earlier. Sometimes this security bullshit can take a while. Especially if the COs on are dicks."

They walked up two flights of stairs and onto a raised, glassed-in walkway. Even over Vanessa chatting about the inner workings of the jail, Elizabeth could hear the muffled call of birds. She thought for a second they might be pigeons, but of course, they were not. This close to the bay, they had to be gulls. They circled over the pods of metal and brick. Elizabeth stopped a moment, looked out the window at the pods, the trees, the gulls. A lone white-and-grey bird hopped around the roof under the walkway on one foot, the other missing, lopped off, perhaps, by razor wire. Vanessa held the steel door open, checking her watch again. Elizabeth stalled at the doorway to take one last look out the window at the sunshine and thought of the Bridge of Sighs she'd seen in Venice years ago where convicts walking from the Doge's palace to the interrogation room would have seen their last piece of Venice before incarceration. She and Vanessa walked quickly down two flights of stairs, through another set of steel doors, and then stood for three minutes in front of the heavy gate, waving at the security camera for the CO to notice them and buzz them through. When he finally did, the door slowly slid across with a mechanical clank and groan. Since the facility was meant to house everyone from petty thieves to rapists and murderers, it was built to maximum-security standards. As the gate shut behind them, the concealed steel bars locked with a clang that echoed against the windowless brick walls. *Here we go,* Elizabeth thought. *Here we fucking go.*

Vanessa tugged at her sleeve, pulled Elizabeth around the enclosed center circle toward the spoke leading down into unit six, and waved her phone-sized Man Down Unit at the CO behind the steel-and-Plexiglas cage she called Central Control. The CO nodded. Elizabeth held hers up too. A light flashed. Another nod. Vanessa clipped the unit to her waistband. Elizabeth, the same.

"I don't know why we bother with these stupid things. Half the time they don't even work."

Elizabeth had been wary of this computerized security system that the program director had so raved about during her interview, skeptical that some infrared sensor unit could track the exact location of staff anywhere in the jail, let alone keep them safe. It sounded too good to be true. She stroked her index finger over the red reflective bar. Man Down Unit. In whose hands had she entrusted her life? These pathetic little plastic rectangles, these so-called technological wonders clipped to everybody's waistbands, were just as unreliable as everything else.

"Oh, great. Phil Collins is in the bubble. I shouldn't say that. He's just such a jerk, always making us wait at the sliders."

Vanessa checked her watch again, took a swig from her water bottle, adjusted her black shoulder bag, and said sarcastically, "Welcome to Georgian Bay Correctional Centre."

"What's the bubble?"

Vanessa pointed through a steel-and-glass sliding door, down a hallway through another steel-and-glass sliding door to a raised, enclosed, glassed-in platform in the center of the pod.

"It's unit control. The CO in charge opens all the doors, watches the security cameras. And who knows what the hell else the guy does. Sits and spins on his thumb in the bubble all day, probably. See him in there?"

Elizabeth squinted, made out a bald head.

"Guess you can't, really. That's Phil Collins. The inmates have nicknames for everyone. Sad thing is I can't even remember his real name. That's so terrible." She covered a smile with her hand. "Wait till you see Harry Potter and Fat Bastard."

The slider at the opposite end of the hall opened slowly. A stream of men—old, young, white, brown, black, Asian, Latino, and every variation in between—shuffled along the corridor toward the two multipurpose rooms. There were receding hairlines, ponytails, bald heads, and Afros, as well as beards, goatees, soul patches, and white rectangular moustaches. Elizabeth could make out neck and hand tattoos, facial piercings plugged with soft plastic. A female correctional officer with long bleached hair walked backward from the inmates toward Vanessa and Elizabeth. Her blue uniform seemed a too-small sausage casing, and as she turned toward them, Elizabeth couldn't help but notice her frosted pink lips and mascara-encrusted eyelashes, the way her chubby rouged cheeks forced her eyes into little blue slits.

"Guess what the inmates call her?"

Elizabeth shrugged.

"Miss Piggy."

The slider opened.

"Hold your head up. Don't look at anyone."

They walked along the hallway lined with men. It was narrow, barely two people wide. At any moment, one of these guys could fling an arm out and grab her throat. Never mind "making a difference," just try not to get killed. She stopped herself; she couldn't afford to think that way. Elizabeth kept her back as straight as if she'd been at the *barre*, glad her decade of ballet training had at long last become useful. She felt every set of eyes lapping her up, inspecting and evaluating her hair, her face, her shoes, her ass. She felt eyes on her ass. She had not known before today that that was even possible. She could smell the tang of body odour, of morning breath, of the stale sweat of unwashed clothes, and *misty mountain manly-man* scented deodorants. It was as though she'd rolled over in bed beside one of them, all of them, and inadvertently inhaled. Underneath the thick brown hair gathered into a bun at the nape of her neck, her ears burned. Fresh Meat. She could see her nickname dancing in a lighted marquee above her head. She was Fresh Meat.

Vanessa and Elizabeth stood outside another entrance, waiting for Phil Collins to unlock the door to the teachers' offices. The inmates did not talk amongst themselves. They stared. They waited. A couple of guys with 'V's shaved into their eyebrows entertained themselves by beatboxing, pursing their lips and slapping their cheeks in jaunty percussive rhythms. Elizabeth thought of the phrase "doing time," thought about patience—about no longer being able to make simple choices, no longer being able to decide whether or not to use the bathroom, whether or not to open a door. Miss Piggy radioed the bubble. The lock popped.

Once they were out of earshot of the inmates and in the row of locked offices with computers and photocopiers, Vanessa spoke quietly. "How was that?"

"I kept thinking *fresh meat*."

"You're in prison now, sweetie, you're *fresh fish*. And don't worry, inmates are just like any other man. Once you're here for a couple of weeks, they'll start looking straight through you like you're a piece of furniture."

Just like any other man. Elizabeth clenched her teeth together, swallowed hard. Why in hell hadn't one of the ten other schools within driving distance hired her? Not so much as a kiss-my-ass, let alone an interview. She'd called every principal and not one had an opening—too many teachers, not enough students. Right. And the prisons are full. The school where she'd given up her contract when Alicia was born hinted, as much as union and contractual obligations would allow, that there might be a maternity leave coming up in the second semester. That was something at least.

Elizabeth shook out her limbs, said, "It's kind of like walking through a gauntlet of stink."

Vanessa laughed and touched Elizabeth's elbow. "I'm gonna like working with you. Hopefully Nancy picked up our keys; otherwise, we have to go on the unit and get them out of the Key Minder, which would really suck. Do you even have a code yet? Never mind. They probably won't have it ready for you for a week. Yes! She did; I see them on the table in her office. Here's your cart."

The steel handle of the cart felt cold on Elizabeth's palms. An elongated wire shopping cart (only with better wheels) brimming with files, books, a plastic box of golf pencils, two simple hand-held sharpeners, and a box of erasers. It was a portable classroom laid bare. Vanessa wheeled quickly in behind and around Elizabeth.

"Don't forget to count pencils and erasers before anyone leaves the room."

In the cream brick hallway behind the multipurpose rooms Elizabeth hesitated for a moment, then steeled herself slowly pushing her cart into her first class: a room full of men in jumpsuits, their faces sallow, washed out by the ghastly hue of the fluorescent lights. She paused, tried to relax. Some inmates had their heads down on desks. Some were slumped in chairs or lounged with long limbs splayed open, some crossed legs in various states. One guy tapped his left foot, another bounced the balls of his feet softly up and down. Elizabeth wrote her name on the white board with an erasable blue marker along with a supposedly inspirational quotation and got on with the business of introducing herself and taking attendance.

A silver-haired man with a teardrop tattoo under his right eye lifted his head from the desk, looked at the board, and read:

"*The beautiful thing about learning is that no one can take it away from you. B.B. King.* Nice quote, Miss."

She looked back at the white board. "I'm glad you like it." She was here, after all; she might as well try.

The first round of attendance was easy enough. Then she had to take a second attendance for the unit count, and then a third more intensive round that required a sheet of paper for each inmate, noting his arrival time and his behaviour, marked by a two-letter code chosen from a list of twelve, and later, a box titled "total contact time" that she'd have to scribble in at the end of class to calculate the minutes each individual had spent. Vanessa called it "ass-in-chair time." The province reimbursed HRTC for their rehabilitation time. Inmates earned money for the company based on time in class and every minute counted. Rehabilitation commodified: welcome to the commonsense revolution.

She passed out the English workbooks that were designed for a variety of independent study levels, mostly grade ten and eleven, as indicated by name and number on the administrative attendance sheet. Elizabeth looked around the room, trying to imagine these guys dressed as they might be in regular life, as though she'd just walked onto a subway car or joined a lengthy queue in the grocery store. Truth was, all these guys would be back on the streets in a couple of years, some less, some in only a few months. Two younger guys approached the desk for pencils. Elizabeth opened the plastic box and pushed it toward them.

The room was quiet save for papers shuffling, pages turning, a few soft murmurs. Several men sat reading *I Heard the Owl Call my Name* by Margaret Craven. A 1967 novel about a young Anglican vicar in an aboriginal village who is dying and needs to learn the meaning of life. Was this the best the ministry could do? Elizabeth walked the perimeter of the room, periodically letting a hand drop to her Man Down Unit to check that it was switched on and that no one had stolen it. She kept one eye on the blue button behind the desk, and, satisfied that she wouldn't be shanked the moment she turned her attention to something else eventually sitting down to review the materials she would later be instructing and marking.

She looked at the phone on the corner of her desk—not a real phone, no outgoing capabilities, only connected to the prison unit controls. Cell phones were forbidden on the floor. Every bit of information, every bit of outside contact, including Alicia's daycare, had to pass through one of those CO's. You didn't even need a high school diploma to be a CO. Not so different from the inmates who sat in front of her. What if Alicia got sick?

A guy with long, coarse, black hair pushed his seat back, and approached the desk area where Elizabeth had set up the books, files, and pencils. He kept his head down avoiding her eyes.

"Hullo, Miss. I just wanted to say that I'm outta here in three weeks, so whatever ya got to learn me, you best get at it."

She looked up at him. Perhaps she looked puzzled, nervous even.

His lips parted. "Don't worry. I won't bite." His open-mouthed smile revealed a black gap in the top gums four teeth wide. She grinned. "Even if I wanted to, I guess I couldn't since I ain't got no teeth. My cellie there said to me after dinner one night that this place is the pits for hygiene. You get a stubby little toothbrush and no floss. He said they should be givin' out dental floss. I said, I don't know about you, but I'll just use a sock."

Elizabeth's spontaneous laughter seemed out of place in the room. It reverberated off the brick walls, echoed back as more of a seal bark. The rest of the class looked up from whatever they were doing or were pretending to be doing. A few of them smiled, some chuckled. The man winked at her and sat back down, thumbing through the pages of his blank, pink exercise book. He must be able to read and write somewhat, or else he would have been screened out and placed into one of Vanessa's basic literacy classes. He must be choosing to do nothing.

She stared at this collection of somebody's children. What in the hell could she possibly teach them that would have any relevance, any value in their lives?

Elizabeth could only do what she could do. She could make the class a pleasant place to be. She could bring them the best of herself. And surely there could be laughter.

EVERYTHING
happens
at
Time

Everything Happens at Tim's

I hate it here. It's so bright. Smells like burnt toast and stupid people.

Yeah, well, you hate everything.

I do not. Just stupid tacky restaurants that serve shitty coffee and yeasty food.

You got a penny or something I can scratch with? So, tell me something you do like.

Here. Dime okay? I like tons of stuff. Palm trees. Salt. Rye and ginger. Neck massages. You scratch weird. Am I going to have to watch you scratch those fucking things for the rest of my life just 'cause you said it's okay I'll pull out, it's okay baby don' worry. I can totally picture you in fifty years lookin' like someone's grandpa in a hideous terry cloth robe and slipper set from Giant Tiger.

You hate the way I scratch? Figures. C'mon lemon number three. Damn. So close. You gonna scratch yours?

Na. Take it. I already got my two strikes for the day. What'll ya do if you win?

Trip to Jamaica all inclusive? Flat screen TV? New truck?

Crib? Down payment on a townhouse? RESP?

Hey! Look at that! I won! We won!

What'd we win? How much? Awe. Five bucks.

C'mon baby, I'll buy you whatever you want. You'll see, every-thing's gonna be all right. Vanilla, chocolate, maple? Apple fritter?

BODILY
FUNCTIONS

Bodily Functions

Found your picture in the snow outside a phone booth tonight. I'll bet that surprises you. I'll bet you'd die if you knew you were lost, if you knew you'd been found. If you only knew someone else held you in her possession. I sure would. Then again, you're not like me, are you. Though, when I strain to see, I think I have a pretty good idea of what your eyes are searching for but have not yet found.

As soon as the tour bus pulled into Ottawa, late as usual, I jumped at the chance to use the phone outside Barrymore's. Wrote Sarah a postcard last week promising to call her today at five, around five I must've said. Five o'clock came and went more than two hours ago. I've been stewing about it all the way since Kitchener. She's gonna be pissed too. As if I have control over the ebb and flow of a band on tour any more than I have control over how much someone will leave her for a tip. It's New Year's Eve and I'm desperate to hang out with somebody normal. Been riding around on that thing since Boxing Day. If I were a fox in a leg hold trap, I'd be chewing my paw off. I'd settle for some fresh air. Anything for a chance of escaping this rock 'n' roll circus of super egos I've unintentionally run away with and joined.

Light as a handful of cigarettes, I hop down bus steps, kick the new sidewalk powder with the toe of my Doc. Martens. Take a deep breath of cold Ottawa air in through my nostrils yearning to twirl across the intersection a la Mary Tyler Moore sans beret. Seriously, how else to put it? I'm free.

"Hey Sarah." I say when she answers the phone." I'm in town. The band's busy settin' up for the show at Barrymore's wanna hang out?"

"Shit, Kirsten. I'm so sorry. I just got a call from my manager, one of our servers is sick and they'll be totally screwed for wait staff if I don't fill in. Sorry. It's New Year's Eve."

"Aaron's got you on the guest list. You can come for free, backstage passes."

"You know I'd love to and I wanna see you but it's New Year's. I just can't say no now, I really need the money."

I would beg. I would say please. Please, please I need someone real, if I thought it would do any good.

Hang up the phone and push through the doors. There you are, lying flat in the snow, slightly fuzzy as I'm sure you were when the picture was taken. You're a breath of fresh air in Polaroid clarity. You'll come with me, safe inside my vest pocket. I pat you softly there overtop my breast.

Back onto the bus I creep, slinking upstairs, hoping not to be noticed. Lorne, the band's agent and manager is busy doing paperwork at the built-in green felt poker table. Suppose I should help with set up. When 'don't want to' becomes so strong it morphs into a tar pit of 'can't' it's time to sit on your ass and have a cigarette. Just *can't* be a *good sport* any longer. Carrying guitars, lugging those horrendously heavy Marshall amps. Leave it to the roadies while I blacken up my lungs a little. No sense having any part of me all pink and innocent. Sit on the brown velour love seat, lean against the window and try, unsuccessfully, to shut the curtains. They say Elvis toured on the same bus. Styx too. Lorne says they should put up a picture of everyone who has ever toured on the bus and fucking charge admission. Course, he also owns the bus. Bought it wholesale from an American dealer he boasts as I nod and feign interest. I'm really thinking that the bus must be pretty old, that I hate the orange and brown patterned curtains. I look at his grey fu manchu and big oval glasses and wonder what the hell he wants me to say. I'm so impressed Lorne. You're so cool. No, no you're not too old to be doing this. You still got it baby. No really, you're my hero.

Meanwhile, I overhear the soundman and guitar tech outside unloading equipment, talking about porn.

"You owe me fifty, Sucker!"

"Betting?" I'm naïve enough to wonder aloud to Lorne.

"They put money on when the guy comes."

Do they really? I mean do they really do that? Show guys coming and everything? Guess I always kind of pictured it a little more Disnified, just a scrunched up orgasmic face with a whole lot of moaning. Seems dumb of me now. Of course, they show *everything* that's why guys like it, no fold left untold, no orifice unprobed.

In high school, my friend Miranda got called a *puck bunny* for dating a hockey player. Band pussy is what the drummer called us once when he thought we were out of earshot. I never meant to be such a tag-a-long. When I first met Aaron, I had no idea he was a professional musician, that he played in a band. Like I know you know from your picture, sometimes things just have this way of happening.

Both our parents have cottages on Big Bear Lake. He told me he was a waiter at the Lodge there. About year and a half ago in August I was floating around the lake in a red canoe minding my own damn business relieved at not having to play crokinole with Uncle Numbnuts when I see this guy waving at me from an aluminum rowboat he'd anchored near the shore.

He stood up in his boat, shouted across the lake at me, *Wanna smoke a joint?* Pretty ballsy not knowing me from Adam, I thought. Ballsy and arrogant and attractive, you know what I mean? Could picture those brown dreadlocks sweeping over my face like some kind of lion having pounced and pinned. He lopped his legs over the sides of the canoe, slipped into the bow facing me and sparked up a fatty. We whiled away the remains of the day's sunshine as it beat down upon us. The heat and the weed and the mutual attraction each a catalyst for the dissolution of our normal boundaries, the revelation of personal truths. Later that night talking at the Windsong Lodge we sat touching each other, touching our paper fish placemats marveling at the pointed beak of the pickerel and sharp teeth of the muskellunge and gazing at the jar of pickled eggs on the bar as we drank rye and cokes in short glasses wondering who in their right mind would eat such an atrocity. Then Aaron did, and as he bit through the white and yellow, he confessed that he'd been watching me, that he'd noticed my green bikini, that he'd always been sweet on strawberry blondes. So I'm sitting there, trying not to look grossed-out by the egg, nor flattered by the compliment, probably red faced and drunk, and all I can envision is horrible images of myself on the dock, on the deck, on the rocks, everyplace I can remember I've ever been at the cottage in my swim suit and I'm picking my bikini bottoms, which have never fitted quite right, out of my ass crack. He leaned into me, and with his briney breath said he didn't really work there said he played guitar. Said he wanted me to like him for him not for his axe. His words not mine. As if I would. You see? He's not like the others. That probably sounds corny, pathetic even, but it's true. At least, I believe it. I have to.

The band and their girlfriends file onto the bus, each having done his or her part to set up. They walk past giving me nods and limp smiles as they shuffle around each other through to the back of the bus. Aaron touches my knee and winks as he passes. Soon they're laughing. Totally don't want to put myself in a position of self-imposed exile so I saunter past the double walled stacks of mortuary coffins, bunks they call them, through to the wood paneled lounge parting heavy brown curtains. The polyester velvet on my skin reeks of smoke and false opulence. Poke my head in through the fabric, pause in time to witness spiky haired Cam, the lead singer, kiss two fingers and press them against a gilt framed photo of Elvis '69 come back special. He runs his fingers through his receding, pseudo-Mohawk, pulls out an unmarked videotape from his sloppy black overcoat. Waves the tape in our eyes as if it's a top hat filled with promises of the night ahead. The film could be anything from *Star Trek's* final episode to full blown bestiality. Either way, I fear.

"You guys won't fucking believe this." He says, the consummate ring master selling I don't know what, self-delusion? I'm not buying his kind of magic. "You have to see it! G.G. Allin, man, a punk legend. He's so fucked up! It's crazy twisted."

And to think, the guy writes lyrics.

Cam says Allin's whole gimmick is performing perverse acts on stage while singing. Something, I'm told, about breaking down the last taboos. Ten of us sit crammed in on laps to ensure our viewing pleasure. We stare, titillated, mesmerized, embarrassed and laughing, what else can we do, as he walks out in front of his audience bare-ass naked, shoves a banana up his ass, then eats it. When he defecates on stage, I wonder if he'll be able to top himself. But don't worry, he does. He eats a mouthful of his own shit then smears the rest of it all over his face like some even more perverse Al Jolson. If there could even be such a thing. I half expect him to crouch down on one knee and belt out, *My dear old Mamie… fucked me dead.* Later, he knocks out two of his teeth with his microphone and refuses to attend his own birthday party barbecue unless his brother can find a *chick* to piss in his mouth. Allin will not be disappointed on his birthday. The pissing, of course, all captured on poorly lit home video in priceless Kodak perpetuity. As are, as luck would have it, the regurgitated hot dogs he spews in chunks and bubbles out from the sides of his mouth as a woman, kneeling over his face her clit ring shimmering in the artificial light, continues to urinate in his mouth to the delight and, perhaps bewilderment, of a kitchen full of party goers. Aside from the occasional muffled, slightly condemning "oh man" from party attendees and bus dwellers, the events unfold without comment. As grey and fuzzy as the people leaning up against the kitchen cabinets, we, all of us are complicit. All of it somehow like a big, fat, slobbering mentally challenged guy who sits next to you on the bus and asks you how's it hanging. You just answer that it's hanging fine and get off when your stop comes around.

Me? I'm just the same. Worse maybe. I'm sitting here totally mesmerized. Silent. Sucked in. Can't take my eyes off it. And although it disgusts me, I've seen it all before. Four summers ago, back in my hometown, I worked at an institution cleaning up after those kind of guys, cleaning those kind of guys. The kind of guys people use to call retards. I know, I know. We're not supposed to say that anymore. It's developmentally delayed, challenged, differently abled. And I try to remember that now, after the fact. So, forgive me. But, man oh man, while I was there, I had to keep some semblance of distance. When I wiped the semen off thirty-five rubber sheeted beds every morning or scrubbed the crusted shit out from between a grown man's hairy buttocks, when I saw a man my father's age masturbate beyond all sense of pleasure until his dick was red and raw, I had to separate them from me. What would you do? Bawl your eyes out in the name of compassion, or puke your guts out in the name of disgust? Either way doesn't matter, there'd still be a puddle of cum to clean up at the end of your shift. It's just as different a world in there as it is on G.G. Allin's stage. You do what have to do, play tricks in your head to survive.

I could tell these band boys stories that would make G.G. Allin seem tame, or at least contrived, but I don't. No one here is terribly interested in what band pussy has to say unless I'm busy strokin'. Egos that is. No, I'm supposed to look good, which I do, and fetch beers, which I don't. Sometimes I catch myself wishing to be heard and not seen. Futile with Cam around. Don't get me wrong it's not that I resent his overbearing charisma, I welcome it. His noisy boorishness takes away the awkward silence that sometimes creeps between us all.

Cam swigs his J.D. straight from the bottle, safe in our knowledge of his alcoholism. Knows we know he's off the Antabuse and hell bent for oblivion. Knows we know he's going to end up with a skull fracture from this latest fall from the proverbial wagon. He doesn't care. He brags, as if he's something special, of their new European CD release.

"We'll be bigger than fucking David Hasselhoff in Germany!" he spits as he speaks, "And you know how those Japs love anything North American. It'll be me and Hello Kitty all over kids' backpacks in no time."

Everyone just keeps on laughing at Cam. Laughing and encouraging and watching him drink and spit.

For a while, the guys pass the time crapping on about *Can Con* and *CRTC* and trying to *make it* south of the border. Why Brian Adams did. Why the Hip didn't. Cam mock masturbates on the *friggin* Americans *who don't know shit from good chocolate.* And everyone just keeps on laughing. To humour him? Or, because they genuinely think he's funny? I've seen this so many times before his antics have grown stale. I've been laughing all night but can hardly remember what it feels like to smile.

Aaron coaxes his arm around me, nuzzles me closer with a kiss and hands me a joint. I don't really feel like getting any higher but it's New Year's Eve and I don't want to be the only party pooper. I inhale and hold hoping that midnight will come a little sooner if I'm not really there.

Someone opens a small vent in the roof, but the smoke keeps clouding. I'm suffocating in the heat and smoke and physical proximity of nine other people. Don't their eyes sting like mine? I want off this bus. But, when the guys leave for sound check, I don't move.

Aaron would love it if I'd get on with the other girlfriends. Talk to them as if our gender instantly makes us kindred allies, as if we are fifties housewives fussing over Tupperware and jiggley Jello salads. So, Tami? How's the stripping? Any pathetic male customers begging for pink? Hey Dawn! Tell me about how beautiful you are, how terrific it is being a model and how your agent still thinks you need to lose five pounds for your Costa Rican swim wear shoot! No seriously I really am interested in your new starvation diet. Wanna share my deep-fried cheese sticks?

And then there's Tina.

How are you, Tina?

"Oh well," she'll say, whining, her eyes all puffy and tilted downwards, black eyeliner about to cascade in mime like tear drops down her face any minute. "You know things are always kind of crazy when you're manic-depressive like me. My Dad died when I was nine, drunk driving. He was the drunk. Do you think David's cheating on me? Has Aaron said anything? What did he say? What do you think he means by that? See the scars on my wrists? I tried to kill myself. I was like so depressed. Thank God for Prozac. Really, my shrink is such a doll." Poor you. Isn't that what she wants me to think, to say? "I'm working at a record store right now but I'm really an artist, not just a shopkeeper. I'm an artist too you know. I'm an artist too." I've never been able to discern what it is that she creates artistically other than living melodramas. But the more she repeats it the more I think she believes she'll will it into being.

Aaron accused me once of being judgmental. Maybe he's right. Maybe I am, but I really don't think so. I mean who am I? Just some girl working at a daycare. Don't you hate it when people define themselves by their occupations? Besides, it's not like I'm going to spend my life there, it's not *who* I am, just what I'm doing right now to make a living. Aaron tells me it's my innocence and sincerity that he fell in love with second, after my hair and green bikini, and that I should never kiss his ass because if he wanted his ego stoked, he'd be with a fan. Buncha sycophants. His words, not mine. And for Aaron, I choke back my sullenness and try to talk to them. I do wish myself different, better able to overcome habits of shyness and insecurity. So, I pour more bourbon and mix in grape Gatorade because it's the only soft drink I can find, and it really doesn't matter now what it tastes like because it's New Year's Eve and if I don't, I won't be any fun.

Still three hours to go before the venue. Craig, the bassist, suggests we go out for a special dinner somewhere, seeing as how it's New Year's Eve and all. Cam takes charge and leads us to a pub off Bank Street. Still can't figure out why we always end up following him like Branch Davidians following Koresh into the flames. Okay, so maybe it's me who is over dramatizing now. But we do follow, and don't get me wrong, there is nothing wrong with pubs it's just that it's New Year's Eve and you're, you know, supposed to go somewhere different than usual.

As it works out, it's still too early for the pub to be busy so we take it upon ourselves to push together three of the square oak tables and gather round. Cam's at the head of the table, surprise, surprise. Wonder how Dawn feels about Cam constantly hogging the limelight. I wish she'd just tell him to shut up. That he's a boring ass.

Our revised seating arrangement unsettles the waiter but out of concern for his tip he adjusts with jocularity, places a pile of menus on the table and leaves us to our choices. Seems he returns in no time. I start to panic; I can't find anything vegetarian on the menu and almost everyone else has ordered. He stares directly at me poised with notepad, sincere about getting everything right. If I don't hurry up people will start rolling their eyes, giving me looks like I'm being difficult. I order Fettuccini Alfredo. We gawk as Cam has his turn and harasses the waiter, making I think, a spectacle out of himself because the restaurant is out of Buffalo shrimp. What are Buffalo shrimp anyway? Big hairy shrimp with horns? What a stupid name. Why doesn't anyone look at Cam like he's being difficult? Like he's holding things up? 'cause, oh no he's Mr. Rock and Roll, Mr. Funny Guy, Mr. Lead Singer. And who the hell am I? Who the hell do I think I am that I deserve two extra minutes? Just a *chick* that's who. A tag-a-long. A dime a dozen. Band pussy.

We drink red wine from Australia and my dinner tastes like white paste on noodles and everyone else eats things smeared in gravy or honey mustard and garlic sauce and I wish, at times, that I could be like them, playing the role of an active participant instead of a silent observer, gnawing on bird's wings and fitting in. Like I wished I could fit in at high school, like I wished I could fit in at birthday parties.

I smile, a good Branch Davidian, and raise my glass to Joel the drummer's toast to hard work, success, Juno nominations, supportive friends and family, nod to management, lots more partying in '93 blah, blah, blah. Obligatory rocker close of, "Fuckin'eh." I can't bear to repeat the inanity and besides while he speaks, I'm busy thinking oddly enough, of G.G. Allin and his hot dogs as I stare straight into the heart of my gluey pasta.

After glasses have tinkled, cheers rounded, proposed good will exchanged, Cam leaps up from the table with a carrot in one hand ranch dressing in the other and mock masturbates again. This time it's kind of funny, I guess. Everyone else seems to think so. I laugh too because it's New Year's Eve and the thought of a thirty-one year old man shouting "Jism" at the top of his lungs in the middle of a restaurant amuses me. Something I could never do. I'm glad to be with them all now. What I mean is, I'm happy that I'm not one of the bemused on-looking outsiders.

Back at Barrymore's, the rest of us sit silent by choice while the guys warm up. I reach into my pocket and there you are smiling at me, just as I left you, all stiff and frozen like a damn Xmas turkey, your fat oval face wedged in the armpit of that stranger. I know you don't know him, you can't fool me. The way you have both arms straight at your sides, the way you politely lean into him but still try to maintain distance, the way you seem only to smile for the camera. I see your red lipstick. I see your gap tooth. I see your sad eyes.

What's your name? It's your turn.

Dawn leans in over my shoulder from the seat behind me.

"Who's that," she asks, wrinkled nose, visible distain.

"I don't know actually. I just found this picture outside a phone booth a little while ago."

She snatches you away and laughs. She can sense the nightclub backdrop; she's got a knack for spotting impending humiliation.

"Looks like this guy had a bad case of one o'clock syndrome," she says and hands you back.

Don't worry about her. You look fine. She's a model you know, obsessed with all things physical, beauty by weight not substance. It's okay. You can tell me everything.

Still, I hope you didn't go home with him. I hope you weren't the last partnerless woman in the bar looking for a shot of self-esteem. Warm drunk affection, false compliments and secrets shared. Cold and awkward in the morning when the liquor shield has worn through leaving you somewhere you never thought you'd be found and daylight, like a misplaced photograph, blasts your dignity all to hell.

What
about
Mind

What About Wind?

Shelia heard the whispers. Unlike most of the persistent things in her life demanding attention, they had become unignorable. *I do bad things. It said. What? Don't believe me? Oh ya, baby, uprooted trees, tornados, cyclones, boats tossed belly up on the shore—all the really big stuff. And what you don't see? Harder to prove, though, have you ever wondered how evil spreads? How thoughts float from one mind, one spirit to the next? I'm the transferor of thoughts. The carrier of lost souls. Spreader of darkness. Careful Shelia, the wind said, I do bad things.*

She shook her head, finished wiping the kitchen table and then rinsed, wrung, and spread the purple microfiber cloth out to dry on the edge of the dish rack.

Tuesday. Shelia finished the laundry, scrubbed the floors, and turned the crock-pot up to high. In half an hour the kids would burst through the door demanding food and television. Noisy squirrels they were, chasing each other through the kitchen and dining room, scolding and arguing about who was faster, who was better, whose cookie biggest. Who had the most nuts stored. She made herself a cup of ginger tea and sat on the porch swing, sun still strong enough to warm the legs of her jeans and tried not to think about the kids choosing to savour instead the last vestige of silence. She noticed a spider dangling from a sticky string in the frame of the swing, but basked in the autumn's rays, paying no mind to webs and wind spinning of any kind until she saw the spider move. It was a big spider, not huge or any-thing, about half the size of a Cheerio, she thought. She marveled as the creature slid down its silk and swung from the top swing post and then back again to the side. Remarkable. A sudden gust arose and blew the spider into her fuzzy nest of hair. She jumped and spilled her tea, shook her hair, and pawed at it and at the rest of her body like some kind of crazed meth head all itchy and jonesing for a fix. Anything to get that spider away from her. Then she heard the wind laughing. She knew it sounded crazy, even then. It wasn't the first time, though. Not by a long shot. The wind spoke to her, directly to her. *I couldn't help myself. And you believe in fate,* he scoffed. *It's me! Here I am around you, outside of you and inside of you, the very breath of you, the life force of the universe.* She followed, in her mind's eye, her breath, the wind tracking in through nose, mouth, lungs, blood—instead of filling her with oxygen he was filling her with poison and then exiting just the way he'd entered. Good God! Shelia thought. He was doing this to everyone! *That mama spider,* he whistled, *it's in your ear.* A ghastly laugh. *I blew it in just as far as I could and filled each egg inside of her with a kiss of charcoal light.* More laughter.

A gust scattered leaves along the wooden decking. Shelia knew it wouldn't be long before the decorative mauve mums in the urns would need to be planted. She set her mug down and brushed the hair from her ear, tugged at her earlobe. The spider? Where was the spider? Her ear felt full as though she'd been swimming and water had plugged it, something was wrong. She couldn't hear out of that ear, suddenly there was just a dull buzzing and it felt like there was something in there squirming. But that was ridiculous. She really was going crazy this time. The wind. My God, Shelia thought, keep it together woman! Then the school bus groaned to a halt and the kids were upon her. Never mind her itching ear, there were mouths to feed and scores to settle.

As the wind-whipped spider crawled deeper and deeper inside the moist, narrow channel of Shelia's ear, it grew hungry and weak. And before that spider starved to death with its abdomen pressed up against the ear canal, she managed to lay hundreds of eggs that wiggled their way through Shelia's brain like sperm into ovum. Or so she imagined anyway, her mind replaying the vision over and over again any time life thought to give her pause.

That night Shelia woke with a horrific pain in her ear. She wondered if she had an ear infection. Toby had had one last month, maybe she'd contracted the same virus. Maybe it was a rare brain tumor. What would happen to the children once she was gone? She saw them in the front pew sad and weeping as the pallbearers hoisted her coffin past. Who on earth could she count on to be her pallbearers? Who would perform the service? She wouldn't want it to be so sad. But it was sad. If she died, how could that not be sad, a young mother dead at 37. She didn't want to die! She rummaged around in the locked toolbox they used as a medicine chest finding eardrops and taking some ibuprofen. But every time she shut her eyes there after, a nightmarish scene would flash unfold. Charlie the family spaniel hung up on a hook and skinned like a side of beef. One of the kids darting out into traffic for a ball at the precise time that young guy in the UPS truck whizzed by. Slicing carrots for supper, or were they thumbs?

Wind doth murder sleep.

The visions persisted. She'd open the chest freezer to take out steaks for dinner and imagine them cut from the ample rump of her husband. She slammed the lid of the deep freeze, a pain still throbbing in the side of her dead ear. The school bus driver, drunk and maniacal, raced the wrong way on the highway, children screamed as it eventually struck a tractor-trailer and careened off a cliff. A black clad prowler lurked behind each door waiting to rape and torture Shelia. Fear clung to every movement, every action, every step. Am I having an anxiety attack, she wondered? Schizophrenia?

With every breath, the thoughts endured. Bath time: they would show her crystalline images of her children slowly lying back and slipping under the water, gurgling to a slow, drowning death. As though watching a horror flick, a scrolling film of terror would play relentlessly: she would park the car and see herself leaving a baby by the parking meter driving off only to remember, gasping and clutching her chest, when she got home. Or in the heat of summer heading into the grocery store, windows up, the dog and children suffocating inside the car turned oven, police officers dragging her bawling through a shudder of camera clicking journalists. Broken wine glasses dripping red wine and blood would repeatedly jab themselves into her eye sockets. Each image destructive and poisonous as though she had nothing good inside her but ice pick thoughts oozing blood and nastiness. And then there were the whispers. It started with the parents at swimming lessons as she stood by her lonesome watching. Or maybe it started that day on the porch with the spider, with the wind. She tried playing music in her ear buds, even switched to an audio book, but the whispers would always be there: the mockery, the criticisms of every tender aspect of herself, her shoddy parenting, each look and glance suspect, admonishing. How they hated her! They thought her less than a worm. She could tell. She'd see it in their eyes and hear their terrible whispering telling her she was ugly and fat, her clothes were cheap and out of fashion. She heard them at the grocery store too, the criticism from others about her cereal and snack food choices, the behaviour of the children, all of these negative comments directed at the impossible failure that was she.

Why couldn't these thoughts be happy and loving and positive? She would try to counter each bruise with its opposite, but it took so much effort, she could barely reach up and take the canned corn off the shelves her eyes teary and the overwhelming shame causing her to shrink to a slumping posture, eyes cast down. Her children would look at her and ask who she was talking to as they saw her lips moving. Oh just myself darling, she'd say and pat a head reassuringly. But what are you saying Mommy? Oh nothing. She'd distract them then by reaching for the peanut butter or a bag of rice or a box of whole wheat penne rigati. It was dismal and soul sucking. She was defeated even by her basic daily tasks. She felt something in her ear and it made her itch. It was itchy all the time. She began taking a sleeping pill before bed to fall asleep the ritual soon progressing to chasing the pill with three fingers of scotch in a crystal glass cloaking its medicinal effects. She fell asleep, sure enough, only to wake with a start in the middle of the night terrified that something had happened to one of her children or the dog—its bright eyes caught in headlights in the middle of the busiest road in town—or that her husband, God forbid, had stopped breathing.

The torment. It was never ending. And in her mind, in the eggs, the darkness sat in wait for each would in turn birth an evil thought. Hundreds of tiny, perfect, horridly detailed thoughts seemingly without end. Hundreds of sleepless nights. Hundreds of befuddled days. How could Shelia explain this to anyone?

A psychotherapist suggested exercise, meditation, rest. Rest, for Christ's sake Shelia! The children were desperate to have their mother back. Her husband urged Shelia to drag herself to the family doctor for more sleeping pills and an anti-depressant. Whatever would make her whole again. A psychiatrist recommended mood specific drugs to alter brain chemistry, cognitive therapy. But there wasn't time for more sleep or more therapy, or a drug addled mind: someone had to feed the children, someone had to walk the dog, check the homework, email the teacher, drive children to karate, gymnastics and swimming lessons, call the dentist, wait at the pharmacy, wipe the sticky crap off the placemats, launder the soiled underpants, groceries, cooking, meal after meal after snack and the complaining. Someone had to listen to all the complaining. Soon, days consisted of handfuls of red pills and blue ones, dazed looks and piled up laundry. And still the egregious visions came.

Isn't nature a wonder.

And when the last egg had finally hatched, Shelia fell sleep. Waking to find the dusty shell of a spider on her pillow and for the first time in nearly a year felt almost well. Eeew, she said, picking the carcass up with a tissue, wonder where that came from.

They never suspect a thing. See, Shelia, I do bad things, had she not been so busy scaring up a decent breakfast for the family she might have heard wind say.

THE
EMPTY
VESSEL

The Empty Vessel

Sometimes, like tonight, times when I'm alone and have drunk so much I can't get drunk at all, I find myself at Evan's door. My frantic, hollow knocks seldom go unheard. He peers at me from between the curtains. Locks unclick, knobs turn, dead bolts slide. He smiles, his arms open wide. I collapse into him, into his warm, small body, and nuzzle lips to neck. He strokes my hand with his thumb and leads me to the darkened bedroom. Though he knows it is sleep I need, it is not sleep I want.

Evan's hands must be magnetic; they seem to draw a fullness from me I hardly know is there. And to his affectionate neck caresses, hands as soft as kid, to his kisses moist and real, I yield. I loosen and unfurl into him. Cupping my shoulder with his right palm, he sweeps the hair with his left up and off my thin, extended neck reminding me of a gentleness that seems so far away. I surrender wholly to him and drop my head, chin to throat, knowing that when my eyes are closed, mind chatter quiet, I love him. But when the touch is broken and skin and skin no longer meet, in the shaming sixty-watt light, I cannot stand the sight of him. Or me.

He eases me upon his bed, upon his pillows, never breaking contact. One hand on me, one hand on his stash, he fills the blown-glass pipe. The flame flickers and burns in the darkness, a ray of joy that's yet to come. Evan fills his lungs and seals my mouth with his, exhaling into me. It is this way with us, him giving me all that he has and me giving him all there is left. He strokes the hair away from my face. I allow his fingertips to caress, following the shape of my forehead, the arch of my brow, the height of my cheekbone. His fingertips move in tender circles on my eyelids. A touch so sincere I wriggle free from the confines of shirt, of clothes. He kneads the nape of my neck, my shoulders, my chest, then kisses me, salty tears on lips. I had not known I was crying. Love me, Evan. Hold me, Evan. And he does.

We share the pipe again. He rolls me onto my stomach and oils his hands. As his unworthy goddess, I lie there, taking all I can. Almond and lavender oils swell the air with scent, and mingle thick, blue-pink with smoke and Zippo flame. When I breathe, the heavy, silken air reminds me of simple, campfire times when happiness seemed to come so easily. And now with Evan's hands warm and smooth upon me, I have never felt more loved, more beautiful, and more vacant.

WHEN THE
FIRE AND THE ROSE
ARE ONE

When the Fire and the Rose are One

Valentine's Day at the Epicurious Café was as soulful as a conversation between candy hearts. Too Cute. Crazy4U. Be Mine. Call Me. Kiss Me. UR Special. And although Laura's always felt a twinge of guilt about her collusion in this elaborate game of pretend, only now has her role as a perpetrator of the great love lie become startlingly clear, gnawing away at her conscience like a twice scorned she-rat. Frankly, she's had enough of the bullshit. But what's a chef to do? Epicurious aims to attract the mainstream customer. Over red wine and cigarettes at the end of the night she and Mary Louise often discuss what people want and how to give more of it to them. They talk themselves into speculative circles that Laura says are like wedding bands, symbolic of eternal futility. And they always arrive at the same conclusion: food and service that is standard and consistent. And for most people that's just the way they like their love too, like their Tim Horton's coffee—regular or double double.

The alarm clock wails, she slaps the snooze button again. Eventually the basement furnace kicks in, marbles dropping into an empty garbage can and then humming. Expectations of the day ahead twist in her gut, propelling her from bed to shower. At least she finished making the beet soup yesterday. It needed that day or so for the flavours to meld, for the lemon grass to infuse the cream and beet puree. It'll be a brilliant valentine's pink with a drizzle of sour cream hearts setting the tone for the meal. Laura had toyed with calling the soup *Beatific Borscht* in honour of the day, Valentine being a saint and all, but after saying it aloud a couple of times it sounded about as romantic as a kick in the nuts. In the end she called it *From Russia with Love*.

Valentine's menus, unlike the love they are meant to sustain, can be well thought out and planned in advance. Sometimes, to make popular dining occasions even more festive, Laura will create a list of thematic specials. This year, she envisions a traditional colour scheme of pink, red, white and bits of green: love with a hint of innocence, and, of course, envy. Keeping theme meals tasty and tasteful, however, means she must walk the line between class with a pinch of kitsch and full-blown tackidom. It was that slippery slope of precise definition; the difference between erotica and pornography, between raw oysters and penis-shaped pasta. Tonight, customers will get exactly what they want: what everyone else is having and love on its best behaviour.

Since Epicurious is the only vegetarian restaurant in town, Laura and Mary Louise know they have a lot to prove. People might dine at the Epicurious Café once out of gastronomic curiosity, but would return if the spinach gnocchi, ambiance, and service were right. For Laura's part, she's made a concerted effort to update the vegetarian menu, replacing bulgur stuffed eggplant with samosas dipped in cilantro chutney and providing meatless versions of popular ethnic foods like sushi and tandoori tofu. And Mary Louise, a master of set design and a consummate two-faced hostess, lures diners in, and through kiss-ass etiquette wiles—perhaps a free round of liqueurs or a complimentary piece of chocolate coconut cream pie—convinces them to return.

Laura kicks the snow from her boots and opens the back door. Is grateful for the silence of the empty kitchen. Soon enough, though, Mary Louise will be buzzing about, pesky as a fly. It isn't that she doesn't like Mary Louise, she just doesn't need her landing on her forearm every five minutes nattering away and interrupting her thoughts. She dumps a soggy filter from the coffee machine, which one of the wait staff should have done the night before and brews a fresh pot. Yesterday's 'Food' section from the newspaper is scattered across the bar. The headline catches her eye. "New Taste Receptor Identified," it screams, like it's the biggest news of the last fifty years. Scientists and chefs have been arguing about the existence of a fifth taste. This fifth taste describes the pungent flavour of food that intensifies and improves by aging or curing like Parmesan cheese, balsamic vinegar, or soya sauce. The Japanese have referred to it for centuries as *umami*. Chefs claim they've always known about it, that a dish isn't complete without all flavour elements: salty, sour, sweet, bitter, and pungent. Western scientists claim to need more quantifiable, empirical evidence before confirming its existence, while for the Japanese, *umami* has come to mean the essence of perfection. Laura sets the newspaper aside, walks past the window toward the counter, thinking how very western to need a legion of scientists to prove what is, perhaps, subjective and unprovable.

She whacks a handful of garlic cloves out of their skins with the flat side of a cleaver, then chops vigorously, creating a hollow echo in the still of the noon kitchen. The lonesome quiet is deceptive. Once seven o'clock hits she'll be tangled in the weeds, alert and hyper-focused on getting orders right. She appreciates being able to dawdle and think about things like tomato okra curry and the nuances of love.

Laura dumps the garlic into the food processor. Of all the silly things, as if that one special, that highest order, that fifth dimension, that *umami* love could ever be done justice by a day of clichéd cards and cinnamon hearts. Picking the leaves off a bunch of cilantro and tossing them in with the garlic, a preliminary to the chutney, she considers her own romantic ineptitude. How many times has she said, I love you, and not really meant it, not the way she was supposed to. What it usually means is that I love that you love me. And how gleefully she has participated in dinners and lovemaking, not really loving the way her partners believed her to love. Well, not in *that* way. Not like *that*. She dribbles olive oil into her cilantro-garlic mixture and delights in the whizzing sound, fury, and violence of it all.

As she stirs tomatoes into olive oil, she thinks about how almost all of her recent lovers have had a thing about tomatoes. It's hard to keep them straight. Robert didn't like tomatoes. Beverly liked them as long as they were smooth and blended into a sauce. Kim didn't mind tomatoes cooked but found the raw ones too acidic. Chris only ate meat, tomatoes therefore, were only indirectly an issue. Janice could stand them as long as they were in the form of Clamato. And, Bill, well, his tastes didn't really count because he covered everything with Louisiana hot sauce, which, incidentally, doesn't contain tomatoes but looks as though it might. And she had loved them all, just not like *that*. Not like she had loved Stephanie.

Louis Armstrong blasts over the speakers: "Birds do it, bees do it. Even educated fleas do it. Let's do it. Let's fall in love…" Startled, Laura nearly burns her forearm on the rim of the pot. Obviously, Mary Louise has arrived and is testing musical content and volume for tonight. Wouldn't want any screw-ups. Guns and Roses screeching, "I used to love her, but I had to kill her." Laura swallows the last of her cold coffee as Mary Louise bursts through the swinging door.

"Oh my God, Laura. I just returned a message and wound up booking a table of eight middle-aged, single women for tonight," she says, hand on hip, eyes wide in disbelief.

"How do you know they're single, maybe they're couples."

"Wouldn't that be great for our image? Why don't we just advertise bra flambé and hang a pair of Birkenstocks on the Epicurious placard?"

You could love her and hate her at the same time.

"Besides, 'Betty' made it very clear that it's a girls' night out. Some kind of lonely-hearts club."

"And the problem is…?"

"The problem is we're going to have eight cackling crows chuffing back margaritas into the wee hours and spoiling the mood for the rest of the clients! Shit. Shit. Shit," she says as she heads back to the dining room. "Where am I going to squeeze in a table of eight?"

She could have said the restaurant was full, but Mary Louise has a head for business. She knows eight birds in the house are worth ten at the door.

Laura strolls through the restaurant admiring the progress Mary Louise has made with the ambiance. Candles, flowers, music, starched white linens, a bud vase with pink and red roses on each table. Laura fondles an outer petal of a rose, forgetting for a second its fragility. Bruises it between her fingers, then lifts a stem to her nose, expecting fragrance but smelling only florist shop. Not like the roses in Great Aunt Edna's garden.

Now there was a woman who appreciated love. Once, after too much vino at Great Aunt Helen's funeral, Edna mourned, at characteristic top volume, *her poor, tragic, spinster sister's loveless life.* Then, during the reception at the back of the funeral home, she grabbed Laura's shoulder and whispered, tears welling in the corners of her hooded eyes: "Well, one thing about my life, dear, unlike Helen's, may God rest her soul, I've certainly been loved. Many men have loved me and I've broken many hearts. But, and I'll only tell this to you, dear. I've only ever really loved one man, and when I think of all the happy times, all the happiness we could have brought each other, I am so sorry and so sad we ever let anything prevent it."

After careful detective work, courtesy of Grandma Jean's big mouth, Laura deduced that Edna's lover had been her lawyer during her second divorce. And horror of all horrors, he'd been married.

The phone rings from the reception alcove. She hears Mary Louise gushing in her singsong oh-so-pleased-to-serve-you voice. "We have a table for two available at nine if that suits you. Wonderful. We'll look forward to seeing you then, Mr. Davis. Happy Valentine's Day to you, too."

Back in the kitchen, Laura collects bittersweet chocolate squares from the pantry, unwraps the foil and places them in a saucepan with a little espresso. Stirring constantly, she adds Grand Mariner to the pan and to her empty coffee mug beside the stove. She can't stop thinking about crazy, old Edna. That same day, after the funeral, after Laura's conversation with Grandma Jean, Edna spat the scotch mint she'd been sucking into a cocktail napkin and breathed the end of the affair into Laura's ear. Leon had phoned Edna, told her to meet him on the steps of the courthouse. He was prepared to leave his family, to begin their future together. It was hard to imagine crinkled old Aunt Edna as a vibrant lover, a mistress even, leading the sort of life of a Hollywood tearjerker. Laura thought the story smelled fishy. If

Grandma Jean hadn't been able to confirm the details, she never would have believed it. But so it was: Edna agreed to meet Leon. And that night, on the way to the courthouse she was broadsided by an oncoming car, her body crumpled in a terrific crash. Providence of course. The two lovers never spoke again, and a couple of years later, Leon was dead of cancer. Grandma Jean said it served him right. Edna said he died of a broken heart. Laura never would have thought twice about the tale, would simply have smiled in sympathetic ignorance and dried the hot old lady breath in her ear with a napkin had she not fallen for Stephanie. But her smile toward Edna and the embrace that followed had been empathetic and knowing of the risk involved when one chooses to make herself as vulnerable as a rose to a hand.

Laura leaves the chocolate mixture stove-side to cool, removes a tray of strawberries from the refrigerator. Washing and slicing, she thinks of the first day she saw Stephanie at the pastry course offered by the local college. Cupid might well have pasted a picture of Laura's bare ass on the bull's eye and let fire.

Stephanie said she took the course to *brush up* on her pastry skills and because she'd recently separated from her partner and needed to *get her head together.* They had resisted nothing. The first night, dinner, then too much red wine, then a six-month *trip to the moon on gossamer wings, just one of those things.* Then she was gone, back to her partner. Left an *I'm sorry for being such a prick card* stuffed under the door of Laura's apartment. Sorry. Another one of those words.

With the skill of a surgeon, Laura cracks and juggles an egg, slipping the yolk into the chocolate and the white into the bowl. And again, crack, juggle, slip. Adds a little salt to her egg whites beating them into froth and folding them into the chocolate and cream. Like Edna, Laura is burdened with having held and lost. The bittersweet chocolate mousse is for them and for the couple who, straining their voices through toothy sieves, can't bring themselves to end it long after the spark has extinguished itself. Most of the time they just constrict and annoy each other until all that's left of love is a lonesome ghost swinging on the door of their empty hearts.

Umami. Love's existence can't be measured like flavours, like lies, like earthquakes. Though maybe, Laura thinks, that's just what the world needs, a polygraph test or Richter scale to chart and confirm love's varying degrees with a printout for verification. Electrodes hooked up to hearts everywhere monitoring the effects of the smallest romantic whim to the aftershocks of the kind of love that finds an eighty-five-year-old woman weeping for a man with whom she never even shared a life, the kind of love that holds a young woman captive, dreaming of her old flame and dripping sour cream hearts into soup in the back of her restaurant on Valentine's Day.

And
Vivian
Said Moo

And Vivian Said Moo

Salty grit from winter road spray stung the corner of her mouth, bit the flesh of her cheek. She spat as discreetly as possible, wiped her mouth on the sleeve of her grey wool cape, careful not to smear her braised berry lipstick. Montreal drivers. She'd barely been off the Metro two minutes and already she'd been slushed. That Denis was living way over in the other end of the city could become inconvenient—if she should be invited to visit more frequently. Vivian had made this trek just once before, and though it'd been a couple of weeks, she basked in the memory allowing it to loop through her mind on continuous replay.

She caught her reflection in the window of a shop selling little communion gowns and veils, dwarfish suits, wall crosses, and other Catholic paraphernalia and checked her teeth for flecks of lipstick. Somehow, she'd managed to do it. She was irresistible.

Last time, before she left the house she'd stood at the mouth of her closet, nearly swallowed up by reams of rejected fabrics jammed onto hooks and hangers, jumbled on top of each other in piles at her feet. Nothing seemed to make her feel as though she had that certain *je ne c'est quoi*. In the end she'd chosen old jeans, a white T-shirt, and a black fitted blazer with the sleeves rolled up—so very chic. Clothes made the woman, after all. So, they said.

This time she wanted to make more of a statement, wear something a little more artsy, something everyone would think looked cool. God forbid she be caught trying too hard, though, showing up over-dressed for, for, whatever it was they would do. If she could only emulate the capricious style of native Montrealers, chunky ashen hairstreaks, layer upon layer of black, bee stung lips lined in claret, the ubiquitous cigarette. From a heap of discards, this time she had selected a snug black turtleneck, slimming black pants, tall black boots, and a long, hand painted silk scarf in tones of lime and leaf. She had looked at herself in the full mirror and concluded, *Voila!* It was all so silly really since she wouldn't be wearing anything for long.

Last time Denis had sat her down on a stool beside an ashtray volcanic in its stature, with a chipped mug of black coffee and a few words about not feeling threatened, that he was indeed a professional. She giggled now with anticipation of what was to come and wondered fleetingly what Graham would think of all this. Never mind about Graham. When was the last time *he'd* admired her as she deserved to be admired. She was beautiful, damn it. Like Denis said, the epitome of womanhood. She was Venus in an oyster half shell, sensual symbolism come to life. Where was Graham anyway? At the foot of her bed gently massaging her feet? Serving her grapes and Camembert? Snuggling up beside her, giving her the time of day or some other offering of self? Hardly.

Away again on 'business' in Vancouver or Toronto. Sure. A little business, a little pleasure. Probably fucking some foolish waitress with a flabby ass, too much make-up, and no opinions of her own. It wouldn't kill him to pick up the phone. It wouldn't kill him to send someone else in his stead. It had been another long three weeks. And it wasn't fair, him gallivanting across the continent and her stuck here in Montreal all alone, where she hardly knew anyone. This, she had not signed up for. Vivian was about to burst. Luckily, she had Denis.

She turned left on St. Laurent, walked with full strides into the damp air, then slowed, fearing she was early. Traced with gloved fingertips a grid of crosses along the mortar between the bricks delaying her approach to Denis' apartment/studio. The door was of industrial steel and used as an entrance for several above-store lofts. With a nervous jab of her index finger, Vivian buzzed.

"*C'est moi,*" she said, leaning into the intercom. She knew *le français.* She also knew she didn't speak it very well despite a hefty vocabulary drilled into her by the Ontario public school system. She preferred, in the company of Quebecois, not to speak it at all. She'd already made *that* mistake. And where she had expected francophone gratitude for her efforts, she experienced only francophone sneers for her ineptitude. Like that waiter who pretended he couldn't understand she was asking for *un sandwich au poulet*. Said, *pardon? You want a chicken sandwich?*

Of course, Denis was only half French and he could never be that cruel. Vivian would let some slip out experimentally a little more each time, spurred on by tender *bon mots* of encouragement. Thoughts of his breath, of his lips hot against her ear.

The buzzer sounded. No verbal reply, just the impolite mechanical groan of the automated door. Vivian sprinted up the first few steps then stalled before his apartment to catch her breath and not appear too eager, though she was eager, dreadfully eager. She longed to be drunk with passion, to twirl across hardwood on toe tips for Denis, enraptured by her goddess-like aura, to swallow her vision, the wonder that is Vivian, completely.

She let herself in, squeezed past shoey clutter, nudged a pathway with the less than delicate toe of her boot.

"Bonjour, Denis."

"Hi," he said, without looking up. A shaggy shock of dirty blonde covering eyes that Vivian knew, from the first time he had removed his dark sunglasses on the street, to be a light amber brown.

Why did he have to be so perfectly bilingual? Never a hint of a lilting ze or dis in his voice. Well, he *had* grown up in Westmount which was about as French as Rosedale. Denis, the prodigal son, always unshaven and rarely clean clothed unless an occasion like family brunch called for it. Conveniently for both, Vivian was charmed by the renegade. She couldn't help but think, though, a slight accent might make him even sexier. As if he could get any sexier.

Denis did not budge from the love seat, his head buried in some trendy magazine with, Vivian saw from across the room, neon yellow typeface made to look like spray-painted graffiti on brick. It was just his way. He was French. He was an artist. She could always use the fifty bucks he flipped her at the end of the session. She unlaced her high black boots with the heavy soles. The lime and leaf silk scarf fell from her neck and melted into a puddle of boot snow on the floor. Vivian always tried to wear something with a bit of green. Someone told her once that it brought out the green in her eyes. Not that Denis would be able to see her eyes from way over there, even if he did look up from his magazine. Perhaps when the lights were dimmed, and she'd arranged herself on the cot.

She took her time approaching him. Knew well enough not to plop down on the love seat beside him. Perched instead on neutral territory: the stool he'd set out for her last time. He finished his article, closed the magazine and looked up.

"Smoke?" He reached down to a soft pack of Marlboro Lights nestled under a heap of squeezed-out tubes and brushes. Vivian accepted. When in Rome…

"What I thought I'd do today, sorry, did you want a coffee or something? Might be a beer in the fridge? You okay with this?"

Of course, she was okay! Did she not look okay? Was all black a mistake? Did she look like a mime? "Oh yeah, fine, my mind's just somewhere else."

"Lie where you did last time. Relax. I'm gonna block out a bit of the background, fill in your figure, try to create the illusion of depth."

He paused, rose from his seat and, moving toward the easel, adjusted the canvas, her body image large upon it. Her voluptuous woman's figure, imperfections she'd loathed her whole life made beautiful by Denis. Made shapely, desirable. At last, someone saw her value. And, without her, he could not finish this piece. Perhaps he'd want to paint more, perhaps a whole series devoted to Vivian: in the bath, in a towel, sleeping in a tangle of sheets. From here their love would blossom; she'd finally have direction and the courage to leave Graham. They'd be caught by the paparazzi holding hands at an art exhibition and be shown in the *who's who* section of some artsy magazine. Vivian's gaze will be downcast, her smile demure, red hair flipped over one shoulder just so, and what would she wear?

Denis handed her a scratchy, brown, terry-cloth robe and pointed to the screen at the side of the room. He appeared not to have noticed her dramatic black outfit at all. Still, she felt sexy slipping naked into this bargain store robe in the stark light of his apartment with him fully clothed. She strolled over to the quilt-covered cot, as gracefully as circumstances allowed, and let the robe drop into a heap at her ankles. Bent at the waist to retrieve it and tossed it over the screen with an insouciant accuracy that suggested it was the sort of thing she did every day of the week. Two could play at this game. Denis draped a burgundy satin sheet around the pillows on the cot and gestured. She cozied in, her heart a purr, sumptuous feline that she was.

What would Graham say if he could see her now? When he saw the finished product hanging inside La Musee Des Beaux Artes? It'd probably never get *that* far but there would be gallery showings, it would end up somewhere—eventually. Worst-case scenario, above some poor sap's mantel. Oh. A naked picture of Vivian hanging on a wall in some stranger's house. Maybe they'd laugh at her. Maybe they'd step back from the canvas, cocktails in hand, pointing out her thick waist, ample hips, and pale nipples. Maybe they'd wonder why Denis had chosen to paint her at all.

"Tilt your head a bit to the left. Lift your chin up. Whoa. Good, good okay. Beautiful."

Yes. She was good. She was beautiful. They wouldn't laugh.

"Cross your legs a bit more so your knee comes up. No. Look at the picture, like we did last time."

Vivian moved her leg up, felt more exposed than previously, less nude, more naked, and wondered if this is what Denis intended.

"Okay, I think I'd like you to bend your other knee just a little more, Vivian, just open your legs a little. Good. Okay now tilt your hip and thigh down towards me. Nice, nice."

Paintbrush fully loaded, he stroked her canvas thigh. Dragged the brush up the length of her torso, past the contour of her breast and along toward her armpit. Vivian imagined that it tickled.

She had first met Denis a couple of months ago though it felt like she'd known him longer. Every day on the way home from her administrative assistant job, she'd walked by the red back door of the art supply shop, and there he'd be, always out beside that door enjoying a cigarette. At first, they tried not to look at each other, to pretend not to notice. Then one day she'd smiled, and he'd said, Hey.

Now, he held her ankle gently with his right hand, slid his left up to her knee and guided her leg to his desired angle. She wished he'd keep on with that touch, slip his hands on both sides of her hip bones up to her breasts and shoulders, hold her face in his hands. A soft lipped kiss.

She'd stopped to talk. They'd laughed about seeing each other every day for weeks before speaking, about how he always came outside for a smoke at the same time, hoping to see her walk past. She had admired the way the deep V of his tight T-shirts showed off the strength of his chest. He invited Vivian to meet him downtown at a club for a drink. She'd declined, failing to mention Graham as her excuse, and turning back, suggested Tuesday for lunch, perhaps, Lou Lou Plastique? He'd been late of course, but as an artist, all was forgiven. They ordered items from an eclectic menu peppered with phrases like global and fusion. They drank black coffee and smoked. Vivian gesticulated pointedly, her borrowed, waving cigarette an extension of her stories about meeting semi-rock stars through Graham.

Then Denis shared an idea he'd been germinating as he watched her walk past each day. He wanted to paint a modern Venus. Vivian's long, red hair and fair skin fit his artist's conception perfectly. Would she consider posing? He'd pay her of course.

Denis put his brush down and approached the cot. Stretched his arms above his head, over each side. A touch at her heel startled. His fingertips trilled along her calf up to the hollow behind her knee. Her skin began to crawl with something quite different from pleasure. For a second, she wondered exactly who it was that she was betraying. He opened his hands and continued caressing the length of her body with open palms. Vivian's back arched. She felt the wet heat of her arousal. Denis winked at her and licked her kneecap. He didn't speak, turned back to the painting and carried on with his work in silence, though he seemed sometimes to stare down between her legs as though considering what she might taste like.

Would he ask her to stay? Would he ask her to brunch with his family on Sunday? Would he hold her gaze with his while she let the corners of her mouth curl up ever so slightly? Would he have a box of condoms in the drawer of that little table beside his bed? When had he last washed his pillowcases? She didn't want to wake up with clogged pores and pimples.

A short time later he sighed audibly. Threw his brushes into a bucket of mineral spirits at the base of the easel. "I'm done. Get dressed," he said, an unlit cigarette juggled in the corner of his mouth.

Already? Weren't they were just getting started? He had touched her. Licked her. What had she done? Vivian obeyed. She was sure the flush of her face was visible through her foundation. She dressed quickly, stepped into her boots, and lingered, practically ignored, green scarf and all, at the front door. Denis scrambled, scoured his pants for crumpled tens and twenties then dug into a bowl of change, sifting through pennies and half-used matchbooks and then through other pants pockets for coins to fill the difference.

"Fifty, right?"

He refused to meet her eyes. Pressed the bills and change into her hand and cornered her by the door. Vivian clutched the money in her left hand and watched helplessly as a dime slipped between her fingers and rolled down the hall, spinning furiously with a metallic echo toward its eventual stop. She stumbled and grabbed for the banister and, as the door clicked shut, thought she heard Denis mutter, "Silly cow."

LOVER'S BRIDGE

Lover's Bridge

Marissa walked along the bridge that crossed the Coldwater River. Real original name, she thought. That's what Thomas Dean had said the first time they'd hiked the trail this far into the woods. This was the way she liked to remember him: witty, handsome, fun loving—alive. The way his brown fringe alternately concealed and revealed one bright flash of blue eye, not all drugged up, drunk, and flailing around in the freezing, rushing water. Suicide they said. Heartbroken, they said. Marissa had no choice on discovering he'd slept with her younger sister. Idiots. Anyone with half a brain ought to know he'd been pushed. She took her hands off the railing, turned, and carried on along her way unable to suppress the start of just a little smile.

a mole to remember

A Mole to Remember
(A new telling of an old folktale...)

These days most agree that a law of cause and effect, of action and reaction governs life. If you're Hindu or Buddhist, you might call it Karma. Jewish, or Christian, a law of divine judgment: you reap what you sow. And nowhere is this principle more glaring than in the tale of Lacey Mae MacLeod who wrote books with all her heart to save young women from libidinous temptation, from the thorny tangle of the devil, and largely, from themselves and the natural sexual curiosity that certain evangelical sects find particularly threatening in a girl. Lacey Mae herself had been troubled once. Maybe twice. And she sought by virtue of this closely guarded, undisclosed experience, and the knowledge that she'd gleaned therein to help others who faced similar troubles through her tales of romantic morality sanctioned, blessed, and encouraged by head preacher and president of the Pearly Gates Ministry and Publishing house, Jacob Bradshaw.

Now you must understand that Lacey Mae was to Christian teens, those capable of reading beyond a grade three level any way, what Lady Gaga was to pop music. Her stories of fallen teens reforming themselves from all manner of drug and alcohol addiction, from lewd and lascivious behaviour, had throngs of adolescent girls weeping and twelve stepping their way toward the Walter Hoving Home for Wayward Girls at their first taste of lemon gin. So popular were these novels throughout the United States Bible Belt and certain other pockets of righteousness the world over, it'd be tempting to say they inspired a cult following, if it didn't seem so blasphemous.

Lacey Mae's biggest hit by far was her *Lavender Hills High* series chronicling the exploits of two angelic, blonde-haired twins who avoid losing their virginity at all costs, in every possible location. They said no at the drive-in and prayed for strength; they said no behind the concession stand at the baseball diamond and prayed for strength. They said no at the beach, no in the backseat of a '67 corvette, no at the malt shop, no in the church basement, no while babysitting cousin Myrna's soundly sleeping baby daughter, and you better believe there was a big fat no on prom night given their father had handed them each purity rings in the name of chastity until they were wed. Sometimes, though not very often, Lacey Mae would allow herself a little laugh, thinking that her male characters must have the bluest balls of any men in the whole of the Christian cannon.

Lacey Mae only wished she had half the strength to resist temptation as did her famous twin characters. For Lacey Mae had a secret. Though she loved to write, though she loved helping make the world a better place, though she believed with every wet, spongy fiber of her heart in Christ's teachings, she knew deep inside the dark well of her licentious soul that she wrote to win the praise and admiration of Jacob Bradshaw, whom she deeply loved. And with whom she had been sleeping since the unprecedented rise of the Lavender Hills series. It wasn't just the fornicating that festered like an undigested communion wafer inside of Lacey Mae late at night while watching previously recorded episodes of *100 Huntley Street*, it was the adultery as well. Yes, Jacob Bradshaw was a married man and, she, practically his concubine.

To say that things had heated up between the two of them considerably was an understatement. Everywhere the twins did not, Lacey Mae and Pastor Jacob did. Even this afternoon, right there on his office desk. It had started innocently enough. An extended lunch here, the brush of a hand there. But now they were becoming brazen, sloppy even. She swore she'd heard his personal assistant Paul's cough followed by the embarrassed click of a door but could not be sure. Jacob had called her into his office, had spoken cautiously of his wife's mounting suspicions of his various mountings when Lacey Mae leapt at him skirt hiked to high heaven like some kind of zoo yard chimp. Only now in retrospect did her face purple from shame.

After she'd freshened up, composed herself and left, Jacob had hailed his right-hand man, Paul. Lacey Mae's days at the Pearly Gates were swiftly coming to a close, unbeknownst to her, of course, for as Jacob stared into the trusting eyes of his assistant, draping his arm over Paul's shoulder he said: "We have a bit of a situation here. We need to let Ms. MacLeod go."

"Go?" asked Paul, his insolent tone and trembling voice betraying his incredulity. "But sir, she's our top selling writer. Do you know how much money she brings in? How on God's great green earth could we ever give any sort of justification for firing her?"

To which Jacob replied, "The Lord giveth and the Lord taketh away." And then, after slapping Paul's back and before closing the heavy wood door behind him, "The internet can do what the devil himself cannot." And so it was that Paul stood there puzzling his way through first the platitude, and then the suggestion, until he fully comprehended what was required of him. Paul was meant to dig up disreputable dirt on Lacey Mae so that Jacob could wield his iron axe of self-righteous recrimination. Paul got straight to work. Though he loved Lacey Mae in his own way and hated ever so much for her to go down with such indignity, he saw what he saw this afternoon on his boss's desk and knew what must be done lest Jacob swing his mighty axe Paul's way. That, he could not abide. No, Lacey Mae had birthed the harlot's broth and in it now she must stew. That night Paul began the first of many Google searches that continued throughout the day and on into the following night. Until he saw, in the faded light of an old VHS tape recently posted on YouTube, what appeared to be a dorm room with a raised arm gripping a door jamb, a swathe of golden hair and a large brown mole under a left breast that was hidden and revealed, hidden and revealed, hidden and revealed in a ghastly rhythm of slapping copulation complete with a husky voice breathlessly crying out in dizzying crescendo, *Lacey Mae, Lacey Mae, Lacey Mae*. The name. The hair. The mole. He had seen it all before in Jacob's office.

As he watched the brief clip that Paul had unearthed, Jacob squirmed among the leather tufts of his office chair. Jeez, thought

Paul, by the disproportionate amount of wrath and seething going on you'd think he himself was without sin. Jacob's voice boomed out of the office, reverberated down the hall piercing straight into the gentle ears of his intended target. Lacey Mae soon stood before him in sensible pumps, her thin ankles knocking nervously together as her eyes fixed to the unsavory monitor show. Can't have sluts like her writing morality tales for teenage girls, Jacob said. Tear soaked and humiliated, Lacey Mae gathered her things and fled. The eyes of the remaining employees, like holy water on Satan, burning her back as she left. Jacob nudged Paul's shoulder as they observed her departure from window of the tenth story building. As she poured her sad, soppy self into the driver's seat, Jacob said, "I owe you one." Paul knew however, that it was he who owed Jacob his due and when the time was right, he would have his just rewards.

Poor Lacey Mae wept and wept until she nearly filled the bathtub in which she sat with salty tears. Understanding Christian forgiveness and judgment like only an insider can, she was well aware that life, as she knew it was over. Ahead lay excommunication and shunning. She may as well be dead. And when all the tears were spent, when she had no more guilt or shame to drip, Lacey Mae decided that she would neither be a plaything, nor a victim any longer. A quick call to her private detective brother landed her a nepotistic spot in the Witness Protection Program under a new name, Pat Abraham. Hollywood, here I come she thought to herself as she packed a lone suitcase of clothing and posted a for sale sign in front of her expensive home.

In the City of Angels, the newly anointed Pat disguised herself with a black blunt cut wig, several risqué peel-on tattoos, and a diamond nose stud. Those who knew her well might have noticed a slight resemblance to the former writer of the Lavender Hills series, but they would have to look awfully closely. And truth be known, everyone who knew Lacey Mae wouldn't be looking for her, they would have assumed she'd have died of shame, or otherwise were afeared of cross-contamination, guilt by association.

It isn't long before Pat Abraham is the hottest new scriptwriter in tinsel town. But it's the latest screenplay, the one about the duplicitous and conniving preacher and president of the Pearly Gates Publishing House that has all the studio executives courting her agent. Her new life amazes her. Just yesterday while sucking down a plate of Pad Thai from the craft services table behind the scenes at one of her productions, she bumped into James Cameron of Titanic fame. And today when she got home from a stroll along the Sunset Strip, a message flashed on her answering machine from the legendary director himself. Could he direct her movie? Shock and awe. Charlize Theron will star as Lacey Mae, George Clooney as Jacob.

At the Oscars that year, Pat with new beau James Cameron at her side, sits on tenterhooks as Meryl Streep slowly extracts the winner of best screenplay from the envelope. As she accepts the award, she is sure to thank God in his mysterious ways and wisdom before hoisting the golden statuette upward where, in the lighting of the theatre's ceiling, the heavens seem to meet the sky and collide into a thousand points of luminescence.

Meanwhile, all the Hollywood hullabaloo reached the offices of the Pearly Gates. And people got to talking as people are wont to do. Rumour had it the story was based on the sordid real–life exploits of one Lacey Mae MacLeod and one Jacob Bradshaw. Murmurs grew so noisy at times, Jacob couldn't hear himself think while he was at work, or even while orating in front of his congregation shaking a fist into the imaginary fires of hell. And for the first time in his career Jacob did something he hoped he'd never have to, he asked Paul to hire a lawyer. He was determined to smite whoever was responsible for such slanderous libel.

When the aggrieved parties met, Jacob sent Paul in his stead. When Pat Abraham, James Cameron, and their team of lawyers arrived, Paul just about fainted but managed to secure an autograph for himself first. He hugged Lacey Mae and apologized for revealing her past, explaining that Jacob had all but forced him. Whispered that Jacob contested her story. That he meant to prove himself a moral and decent man, that the script exposing details of his creative bookkeeping and sexual escapades were all lies. Then Paul passed Lacey Mae his phone, which contained among other classified photographs, a sensitive video clip of the afternoon upon the desk from several years ago. Pat Abraham and James Cameron knew just what to do.

The very next Sunday as Jacob sermonized in front of an increasingly large congregation gathered to see the alleged man from the movie, Pat and James projected the lovemaking tape of Lacey Mae and Jacob in high definition behind the alter the full height of the wall. And as he was admonishing the sinners who slunk among them, Jacob's voice croaked to a halt. Pat watched as his face fell, his cheeks swelling with red. For in that instant, the whole of the congregation saw Jacob with his pants to his knees, the blonde back of Lacey Mae's head and the black-brown spot underneath her bouncing left breast. But it wasn't until Lacey Mae stood aside Jacob, tore her wig from her head, her shirt from her chest that the bare breasted mole was exposed in the flesh and the true nature of the events revealed. A collective gasp echoed throughout the nave and a flock of faces stared back at her one face of righteous hypocrisy. It was then that Jacob's wife stood and screamed. The ladies' auxiliary dropped trays of neatly cut egg and tuna fish salad sandwiches. People who normally only spoke in tongues managed to find the word charlatan on their lips and spoke it freely as though it came through from the Lord himself. Thus marked the end of one miserable marriage, one very prosperous career in preaching and publishing, and all in the crowd that day agreed, Lacey Mae's was surely a mole to remember.

In the
of
Time
useful
consciousness

In the Time of Useful Consciousness

It's the end of May. The backyard maples drop green keys into the pool, they spin in the air before landing and floating on the water. My neighbour's apple tree droops over our back fence and is swollen white with blossoms. These, too, will end up face down in the pool. I should probably be out skimming the surface before everything sinks and turns to a pile of crud at the bottom of the deep end that will have to be vacuumed up and will take much more effort in the end. Instead, I watch through the sunlit kitchen window as they fall through lacey shadows, chipmunks and birds flitting and jumping roof to branch, branch to roof. And to think, it was just last year when John and I stood here listening to the noises overhead, the pattering of little feet on the roof, looking out, sipping water, talking. The smell of lilac from the dwarf shrub at the back gate wafts through the open screen, and in my periphery, the yellow rose bush at the side of the deck is once again heavy with buds.

We were here at the sink looking out when a plane flew overhead. John held his phone to the ceiling and said, according to his pilot's app, it's a J3, the oldest plane he'd ever flown. He searched some images of the Piper J3 Cub to show me: a fabric-covered monoplane painted bright yellow. The yellow, with its black voltage stripe, made me think of Charlie Brown's sweater. It's kind of a Charlie Brown plane, I said. John smiled agreeing. My grandpa used to barnstorm in a Gipsy Moth, I added, refilling my glass from the tap. That's how he lost his hearing and couldn't fly in the war, one of his life's disappointments. My grandma was always yelling at him to put in his hearing aid. I imitated the way she used to screech his name: Biiiill! John laughed, said barnstorming took balls, explained that De Havilland made a series of open cockpit biplanes: Gipsy Moth, Tiger Moth, Fox Moth. Imagine being upset that you couldn't go to war, I said.

John said his grandfather was a pilot too, before working in finance on Bay Street, shot down over occupied France and hidden in a cave by the resistance finally escaping by swimming out to a boat in the ocean in the middle of the night. Can you imagine having that kind of courage, he asked.

My grandpa eventually became a florist, I told him, with greenhouses and fields full of flowers, a chain of shops. My grandparents were always going to floral conferences in Hong Kong and Japan because of his interest in Ikebana. I pointed to my inheritance: the Fu Dogs on the bookshelf, the red and black silk robe I was wearing, the white Japanese lamp with cut outs lined with rice paper, a bulb in its base speckling the wall with a pattern of light like frost on a windowpane.

I told him about Ikebana too—the Japanese art of flower arranging that aims to unify humans and nature. Instead of a big bouquet of blooms, I said, Ikebana arranges sticks, seedpods, leaves, and flowers to create a living mediation on oneness. Kind of like you can appreciate each in its individual state of being, but it's the artful arrangement of seemingly disparate parts that creates a profound experience where you consider how the fragments inform the whole. These are the things I taught John. He taught me to look up, away from the earth, to watch the way white vapour trails intersect the blue sky. And as we stood there at the sink, he cradled my face in his hands like a man from a different time, like a heartthrob in a tailored suit from a black and white movie. I tilted my head up to him, he kissed me and said you're so interesting, said I'm so in love with you, and pulled me to the floor of the kitchen where we made love for the second time that day.

When he was gone, off some place I could only dream of going like Santiago or Copenhagen, Tel Aviv or even, let's face it, London, I'd be perpetually distracted. I'd check my phone for texts like a boy-crazed teen desperate for any hint of flirtation. Every heart, every I love you, every kissy-faced emoji sent the dopamine flooding. At my age, I had to laugh. Head in clouds, I'd further procrastinate at work scrolling vegan recipes, celebrity gossip, spring fashions, interesting plays John and I might see in Toronto when he'd next be around. I examined dates. Maybe there would be time for a restaurant. Between John's work and kids' schedule and my job and kids' schedule, our time together was coveted. Had I been able to see him every second of every day it would not have been enough. There we were, already a year in. And I won't lie. I won't say I didn't wonder where our relationship was heading.

My husband and I separated about eight months before I met John. Ending a marriage is never painless. Especially when it persists beyond the date of expiration becoming a cruel test of endurance, for somebody's sake, followed by the heart aching relief of when you just admit your failure, and sit on the side of the road gasping for air miles from the finish line. Though, it's a breaking open as much as a breaking apart. And, in that broken space, if you are very gentle with yourself and others, there becomes room for something else to grow.

After my husband moved out and started taking the kids for his requisite Wednesday nights and every other weekend, I suddenly found myself with free time, a commodity previously reserved only for him throughout the course of our marriage. What did I even want to do with my hard won newly found free time? I mean one day you're forty-something and you realize you've spent your whole life being contorted by everybody else's expectations and your self is little more than the misshapen foot of a bound bride. So, you slowly unfurl the binding and force yourself to learn to walk again on what's left of your feet.

I pretty much threw myself into yoga. If one could, conceivably, do such a thing. It seemed more productive than the wine I'd been numbing with for years. I was looking for fitness, for connection, for growth, but it was the breathing that hooked me. Pranayama: breath control, the breathing in and out of vital energy. Each inhalation is supposed to nourish cells, each exhalation to release stale emotions and physical toxins. How little attention we pay to something so essential to our existence. In class, we'd sync our movements with our breaths, the abdomens of the whole group rising and falling in unison as though we were one organism. Our instructor would say, each breath makes space in the heart. And I'd imagine the air filling my chest and forcing aside and pushing out all the sludge it had accumulated. How many years had I spent shallow breathing? Barely breathing at all? One day, lying there on a smelly mat on a gym floor in the dark "just breathing" I bawled my eyes out, in public, simultaneously dissolving and then becoming whole. Later in the week I had lunch with a friend I'd known for twenty years who said unprompted that I looked like I had my old sparkle back. And then I met John.

One night he'd just returned home from France and came knocking at my door at one a.m. in his pilot's uniform with a bag full of cheese. We kissed at the bottom of the staircase, whispering sweet everythings, then he carried me up to bed. When we were lying there afterwards, he was talking about wanting to buy, or maybe just have a look at, a Piper Cub, a J3, the Charlie Brown plane we heard outside while we were in the kitchen that day. Said there's one for sale in Tillsonburg he was considering taking a look at. If you're not too busy, you could come with on Saturday to check it out, he said. How could I be too busy to go flying with you? I said. He turned to me pressing his forehead against mine, said he could imagine living here, in my house, his things in the wardrobe on the left. He liked the paintings I'd done, the pictures by my kids and of my kids. Loved my two quirky dogs, both desperately in need of grooming. I can imagine it too, I said. We held each other both hoping a life together would one day be possible. The times between moved too slowly and when were together, too fast.

On a Saturday that my kids were at their dad's, John pulled up in his vintage, convertible Jaguar. I had on this scarf of my grandmother's tied around my hair and wore big black Joan Didion sunglasses. John laughed. Snapped a photo. I loved the way he laughed. It started slow and kind of chuckley turning into a full-bodied yuk. His smile was big too, his teeth straight and white. I reached over my head, arms outstretched where the roof would be, and sang a line from Stompin' Tom Conners' Tillsonburg as we sped off towards the county airport with the wind and the sun and the two of us playing at characters in our own little romcom. Top down, clear air rushing, really living finally felt possible. He pulled his blue and white Piper Cherokee out of the hanger. Tested the headsets, repeated emergency instructions for me in case of the worst: Fire extinguisher, door opening procedure (reach up turn lever), ELT device. Gave radio information to someone: Echo, Sierra, Quebec, Zulu. I waited and watched contemplating the origins of the aviation alphabet until we taxied down the runway, took off and leveled out. I wrapped my left arm around his neck, my right around his middle. He was wearing sunglasses, his light brown hair rumpled on top. We didn't talk much, the green headsets rather inefficient for communicating more than simple phrases, but we touched a lot and looked in each other's eyes. I rubbed his neck. Trailed my fingers up his thigh, I might have licked his ear.

An hour and some later in Tillsonburg, we met an old man at hanger five. He was a John too, short though, with hands all crippled into hooks. His faded blue jeans were too big and held around his humpty dumpty with a belt. We didn't shake hands, but he looked at us warmly and invited us forward into the open hanger with a point of his claw. The J3 awaited inspection. The first thing I thought when I saw it was, *I had a farm in Africa.* I know that's a different plane, from a different era, a biplane even, but this one looked old enough and yellow enough that Denys and Karen might have donned their goggles and flown it all the way out of Africa and I suppose truth be told, I day dreamed, I heart dreamed a little while John and John talked J3s. Then my John—*my John*—climbed into the rear seat and the other John motioned for me to join him in the front. I grabbed hold of the wing struts, raised myself up and slid into the front side seat easy like Sunday morning. The Johns looked at each other and laughed. The old man said if my wife could do that, I would have kept her around. Old men and their wife talk. He thought I was John's wife.

On nights when John wasn't with me, I read. I read a lot, it seemed. Had just closed the cover on Patti Smith's *M Train* at one point. Her beloved husband Fred, early on in their marriage, learned to fly and ultimately bought himself the same kind of plane that John had, a Piper Cherokee. I wondered about Patti and her loneliness, Fred long dead, kids gone with lives of their own, her rambling around her apartment in New York, traipsing between coffee shops writing. Poetry sprouting from the backs of receipts and napkins at café 'Ino. Reading her poems, I sometimes I feel as though I could be her sister in quiet melancholy, the two of us staring through apartment windows into our own ennui, running our fingers through the dusty detritus of the past, holding on to irrelevant relics, holding on to what was already lost. How could she not want a man beside her in bed, inside of her in bed? The feel of someone else's skin on her skin, warm breath on her neck, the palpating heart of another at her ear, love's gasping grasp—to be desired? Or was her love and devotion to Fred so singular that no one else would ever do?

When I told my hairdresser that John and I had started seeing each other, she gave me the number of an "intuitive" or a "psychic" and told me to book an appointment. I'd never been to a psychic. So, on a warm Wednesday night in late October, John working somewhere far away, I booked an appointment with Marsha. I drove along Georgian Bay, through apple harvest country, pies and pumpkin stands, autumn leaves and billboards advertising Honey Crisps and local ciders until I got to a bayside motel. Room number 6. Marsha greeted me at the door in a turquoise Mumu aflutter with monarchs, took hold of both my wrists, ushered me in. On a TV tray between two chairs, she laid out my tarot cards proclaiming that all my days of conflict (swords) were behind me, that abundance (cups) was ahead. That I am the Empress and my life was changing as I had been put upon a shelf but am no longer. She took out a pad of paper and scrawled furiously in blue ballpoint pen. She said of my former husband, who's the Taurus? And then she began coughing and clutching at her chest, gasping for air and asking, who is Anne?

Who died of emphysema or some other lung ailment? After determining, I'll admit with some skepticism, that my friend's mother (who died of lung cancer three years prior) had co-opted my psychic reading (the same friend who said the thing about the sparkle), Marsha assured me all my hopes and dreams for the future would hold true: I would be loved and pampered, I would be financially comfortable, I would achieve my career goals. Then, out of nowhere, when it seemed she was winding down, she said, who's the police officer? I could think of no connection. She faltered, eyes gazing toward the motel ceiling, firefighter? No, wait, she said, pilot? A smile burst through me. Wow, she said, I felt such a strong pull of energy around you when I said that. That's how obvious I was. It's funny though, she said, I don't see you together. And I didn't even care. What could she have known of our love?

John arrived just before midnight from Columbia his arms full of flowers. I was trying to get them in water when he grabbed me and kissed me and they fell to the ground. Calla lilies, alstroemeria, weird lobster claw like things, birds of paradise, bouquets of small white flowers whose fragrance filled the house. I fussed around with vases while he rolled his suitcase and flight bag in from the car. Then we scurried downstairs to the basement rec room so as not to wake my sleeping children. It wasn't ideal, but we'd decided not to involve our children at this point as such knowledge of our goings on would eventually percolate through them and to our ex-spouses, and who needed that at a time like this? The pullout couch was excruciating, springs knuckled into our backs, the mattress gone to its own hell of mouse shit and popcorn kernels. Still, I rolled into his arms and rested my head on his chest, and we managed a few hours sleep setting the alarm so he could be up and out before they woke. The mattress, the sleep deprivation—all worth it. Whoever would have thought that there'd be a love strong enough to knock the wind out of us?

In 2010 the Museum of Modern Art in New York City featured the work of artist Marina Abramovic. She would sit on a chair in a long red, black or white gown across from some visitor or patron or whatever you want to call them. They would stare silently at one another, breathing together for a few minutes while gazing into each other's eyes. Often, participants would begin to cry. Abramovic said at the time, tucking her long black hair behind her ears, that no one believed people would come to sit in silence with her, and yet, every day for months on end they lined up and waited and sat, hungry for an emotional experience. She pointed to the need for deeper human connections, for another to be our mirror. Suppose the work of any artist could be the go between, maybe like the reflected light of the moon. Maybe we're all suns and moons. It wasn't until after Abramovic had put in seven hundred plus hours that the scientists' interest finally peaked, and they asked if she'd repeat the experiment in a controlled environment while wearing brain-scanning equipment. She agreed and now ensconced in some digital filing cabinet there is data proving the existence of shared brain waves, a shifting of energy between people.

Last Christmas, we opened presents and had special dinners with our kids on the 23rd and 24th before shipping them off to their other parents for their first Christmases without us. I thought I might feel sad and kind of lonely, but it was just the opposite. The lightness of being out from under the burden of Christmas was such a sweet relief. John and I spent our freedom flying. Cumulous clouds like big breaths of cold air from a snowy, ethereal creature's mouth suctioned all around us swallowing the Cherokee in flight. The inside of a cloud is colder than the sky around and it rocks an engulfed plane. Just when it seemed we were coming through the other side, John tipped dramatically and circled back bursting through and into the obscuring clouds once more. I held onto his arm looking at him and out the window thinking of all the people down there lost in their little living room lives, eyes locked on screens too afraid to look up and around. I might very well have been doing the same if not for John. Up in the air we were free, encased in our own secret, silent world, holding hands unseen. I looked through John's sunglasses knowing he could see in the deepest parts of me his self reflected. Being up there with him was like the moment in time when a droplet of water freezes and becomes a snowflake suspended and glorious with intricate patterns of singularity.

John returned from Tokyo exhausted and smelling of cigarettes. There were bags under his eyes, and he was upset by the bombing at the Istanbul airport. He said he use to land there all the time. That, and some colleagues flying from Milan experienced a rapid depressurization situation where their TUC was reduced, and they had to use the oxygen masks. It's scary, said John. He explained the acronym: *Time of Useful Consciousness*, those 6-9 seconds while the pilot is still lucid enough to make decisions when facing an impending inadequate oxygen supply. That's not very long, I said. No, he said, it's not.

In February, we took our kids skiing. They seemed to have fun. Now that word of us was out, John's former wife always seemed to be at him for something. Before she agreed to the coming year's parenting plan, she had her lawyer add a clause that prohibited their children from being around John's "new partner" until a child psychologist has given stamped approval. It was nonsense of course but cost John to counter. We nick named her the Double Black Diamond, extra difficult, to speak in code in front of the kids. We could not understand why she wanted to waste so much time and life being angry and blaming us for her own failures and unhappiness. Eventually we just said, the DBD.

Summer: white vans plowed into boulevards full of people all over Europe in the name of ISIS. Donald Trump as much as condoned the behaviour of some white supremacists in Charlottesville. The weather was rainy and cool and in our small city north of Toronto the city council decided to eradicate the scourge of Emerald Ash Borer, an invasive species from Asia that had begun to infest cottage country. Ash trees all around our neighbourhood were cut and sliced, the whir of chainsaws, men on ladder trucks, branches of mature ash trees slamming to the ground, the steady hum of the woodchipper all day long, sawdust in the air like sand. The city left the trees with their hacked off branches standing wounded sentinels reminding us constantly of all that was lost. And John and I on the deck, slapped mosquitos and drank Beaujolais, agreeing that we both knew what it took to wreck a marriage.

In 1914 to lessen the chances of pilot fatigue on long flights, Lawrence Sperry invented autopilot, which he's said to have demonstrated by walking on the wing of a plane in the air. He's also said to have invented the-mile-high club. On one adventure, he and his divorcee friend, Mrs. So and So, apparently knocked the controls askew midflight sending the plane plummeting to the water where the pair, found naked, were rescued by duck hunters. Explaining the absence of clothes, Sperry claimed that the force of landing so rapidly on water stripped their clothes right off. What John and I did, and who put what where in such a cramped space while flying on autopilot into the sunset late one August evening, was, as they say, no one's business but our own.

In September, John bought the Cub and we began serious discussions about merging families. We debated the pros and cons of renovating my house versus purchasing a new place that fit us all. We met with a contractor; blueprints were drawn. John flew in from Bogotá late one night, climbed into bed and clasped an emerald necklace around my neck. Later in the week I was driving somewhere, probably had just dropped one of the kids at swimming lessons and got to wondering how I had survived so long without love when that cheesy 1978 song from Sweet, *Love is Like Oxygen*, came on the radio. I smiled. It was almost like I'd had some kind of religious conversion and was born again anew.

We took the Cub to a "fly in," an event where small plane pilots converge on a rural airport, drink coffee, eat barbequed hamburgers and admire each other's aircraft. John's enthusiasm was infectious; I was actually interested in learning. He took my hand and pointed to a Cessna. See, look at the wings, they're top mounted unlike the low wings of the Cherokee. We walked the strip. Blue sky, white smoke and clouds, the smell of fuel and barbeque, the yellow Cub on green grass. Planes flew in and landed. Planes accelerated and took off. Look at the Ercoupe, see the dual rudder? Check out the Bonanza, it's also made by Piper, that's what Buddy Holly was in when his plane crashed. Then came the Harvards, big yellow WWII planes with red radial engines. It was a new language for me, these planes, this love.

And then two weeks later, like a message written in the sky, everything evaporated. John flew the Cub north to meet with a real estate agent in the hopes of buying a cottage on Lake Enid. He was supposed to be home for dinner. When he hadn't texted me by 6:30, I should have known something was wrong. I tracked down the real estate agent. She said John never showed. She said she texted him a few times from the airport where they were supposed to meet before returning to the office. I only had the one number, she said, I texted, I called. She repeated this phrase several times as though she thought I might think she should have done more. I called emergency services, the airport, the police. They contacted the military. Someone flew out and located his transmitter. Someone called me. The next morning, a crew searching Lake Enid found the Cub—found John. The engine had failed. He landed on the water just as sure as Scully, but the small craft flipped and sank and he might have had a chance if not for the tangle of straps that held him in place ensuring he was unable, in the time available after impact, to swim up for air.

We don't see his kids anymore, maybe just a wave Saturday morning at the soccer dome. At John's celebration of life (what we use to call a funeral) they sat at the front with all the pilots in uniform alongside the Double Black Diamond who still bears his name and now his inheritance. John would have hated that. Her at the front of everything representing him. Her in charge of his legacy. I wish I could have stood up and said something, done

something. But I hardly knew his friends let alone his work colleagues and anyway, that would have been for me. Who was I to
influence John's posterity? When she saw me, the DBD sneered
at my necklace, and I wondered how she knew and why she
cared so much now that John was gone and she had his everything. But, of course, John hadn't gotten around to changing his
will, so she was probably dealing with his estate and saw the Visa
bill from Bogotá. His kids moved to hug me; she pulled them in
toward her sour face.

By the time I summoned the courage to use my key to
John's place, the DBD and her friends had it gutted. Pictures of
WWII planes down, models gone, flying books removed from
shelves and boxed, our photos and love letters gone through and
trashed, three black garbage bags stuffed with clothes up against
the living room wall. I opened one and extracted a plaid flannel
I knew well. I held his shirt to my face inhaling him and a David
Byrne lyric came to mind: *I'm breathing in and breathing out, like
humans do. I'm aching and I'm breaking and I'm shaking like humans
do.* How do you go on breathing when your oxygen is gone?

I guess you just do.

When we were kids, every time we'd pass a graveyard, we'd
hold our breath so that the dead could breathe. I played a game
with myself over the winter: whenever I heard a plane overhead,
I held my breath and thought of John up there, his spirit frozen
for eternity like a petrified snowflake hitching a ride on some jet's
vapour trail, or maybe bobbing in amongst the stars just the way
he would have wanted.

Wandering through a thrift store a few weeks ago, as I do, I
found a shallow, rust coloured bowl with a block of florist's
foam. I wanted to make something for John. For me. For us.
Walking around my yard, I collected items to arrange in the
bowl; I considered the maple keys, the fecund rose bush, the
ferns along the backyard fence full as ever, some curled, some

opened. I covered the foam with moss from a neglected part of the hosta garden and set it in the centre of the bowl. Stabbed in a twig from the lilac tree with a gnarled twist that curved to the right. Added a fern frond open and curving to the left. In the middle, a trio of roses on a thorny stem each blossom in a state of becoming: the tightly closed bud, the beginning to open bud and the bloom that threatened to drop its yellow petals at any moment. I placed the arrangement on my kitchen table and there it sat until the roses shed, the fern drooped and browned beyond all hope, and I had no choice but to sweep it all into the compost and start again.

SWAN
SONG

Swan Song

The rain pelted Julia's face. She was most bothered by the way the rain, now turning to sleet, covered her prescription sunglasses obscuring her vision. Eventually she took the glasses off and zipped them into the pocket of her magenta jacket with the reflective stripes that Harris and the kids had given her for Mother's Day. Poor Cuthbert their Golden doodle was sopping wet, belly full of road grit. Even so, she refused to retreat. Once she was clear out of the subdivision and into the wooded trail around the lake where she was pretty sure she was alone, she let out a scream. It began shrilly and trailed off into something deep and guttural. It sounded fierce and ugly when she heard the echo. Primal almost, and it surprised her. Julia looked around embarrassed. She needn't have worried; there was only Cuthbert and the quizzical tilt of his head.

With each stride she imagined in her mind's eye, her legs lifting up, bending, slapping down each fuchsia Mizuno, one after other, harder and faster. Her red nails dug into her palms as she clenched her fingers into fists pumping and propelling her forward into somewhere, anywhere, not here. She was breathing deeply now, sucking in all available oxygen and remembering nights in Ibiza, high on ecstasy dancing in a zebra bikini, not really caring where the mischief would take her. A full moon rave in Bali when she and some other backpackers had been rounded up by the police for smoking pot and thrown in an Indonesian jail and never once had she despaired knowing that Uri, the Israeli she'd collected would somehow find a way to bail her out. She remembered, too, collapsing at the Matador, an after-hours club in Toronto, where strung out on cocaine and vodka and Red Bull, she'd been hospitalized first in Urgent Care and then in the Psych ward. Her parents' faces twisted by worry, disappointment. And it was not long after that that she met Harris.

Her day, divided into short increments of time, never seemed to be her own. And now she'd run too far. She had at this moment, exactly 33 minutes to get to the bus stop to pick up the kids. 35 if the bus was late. 31 if the bus was early. If she wasn't there, it would take the kids right back to school. And then they'd probably call Harris, assuming something must have happened to her. And then Harris would call her all annoyed and flustered because of the distraction from his patients. There was nothing to do now but turn back and run. If she ran full steam, she might make it.

But Julia stopped. She looked at the water. There were swans, five of them swimming on the lake. In spite of the sleet, which had lessened, the surface was calm, save for the quiet puckering of drops. She slipped her shoes off first. Then her socks. She tucked the socks into the shoes and set them neatly beside a bush as though she would be coming back. The jacket was next, then the tights, then the shirt, and sports bra. These she didn't fold but let fall like an old skin into a heap overtop her shoes. She walked into the cold water until consumed. Swam underneath a pair of swans watching orange feet paddle before grabbing onto a foot from each of them. They thrashed their wings against the water and began to rise. Julia held on as they flew up into the fog filled sky their white wings flapping, Cuthbert's barks echoing in the distance, as her small and ever smaller body dangled and was swept away as though the birds carried nothing more than a pasty, pink just caught frog.

OR

[1] Julia runs to the bus stop just in time, pastes a smile on her face and, once home, fixes the kids a snack. After helping them with homework and cooking a healthy dinner, she pours herself three fingers of vodka with a splash of cranberry juice to quell her mind. They watch an inane animated program until Harris swoops in, having avoided the broccoli and homework fights and

heroically puts them to bed while Julia takes a diazepam to fall asleep only to do it all again tomorrow and the next day and the day after that until her liver explodes.

OR

[2] Julia stops by the water and watches the swans before heading directly to the school to fetch the children. She apologizes profusely to everyone for her lack of perfection. After putting the kids to bed, folding the laundry, and cleaning the house, she sticks a fork in the toaster.

OR

[3] She enrolls in a local community college to get an accounting diploma so that she can take over the books for Harris' dental practice. Then, late one night while puzzling over spread sheets and numbers and huffing nitrous oxide, she tears all the financial statements into little pieces and swallows them eventually choking to death on the dry bolus of paper.

OR

[4] Taking her yoga practice to the nth degree, she perfects her bow pose. Unfortunately, one day she pulls too hard on her ankles snapping both of her hamstrings and bleeding out on the beige Berber in the basement.

OR

[5] She throws herself into scrapbooking as a creative hobby. Wednesday evenings she convenes with a group of boring, plump women donning Northern Reflections sweatshirts and vests and talking about children and TV shows while chronicling the life of her family. Upon realizing it has been her lot to stand in the wings, she returns home and late one night after her family is asleep, she puts on a yellow slicker, climbs into the bath tub

like the rapist in the *Dead Zone* and shoves the longest, sharpest scrapbooking scissors down her throat effectively severing a major artery but containing all the blood neatly so that the bathtub can easily be wiped down and the raincoat reused—by the next miserable fool Harris found to replace her. It wouldn't be hard, she was, after all, just an interchangeable cog of womanhood, a supper-making, kid looking after, sperm receptacle.

OR

6 Julia confesses to Harris that she's having some mental health troubles. He rolls his eyes and checks online to see if their benefits plan covers having a crazy wife. He tells her to call their doctor and deal with it. She does. She sees a therapist and psychiatrist every week for two months. The therapist tells her she needs to be more grateful for having such a wonderful husband and four healthy children. The psychiatrist tells her she needs medication to balance her brain chemicals. Harris agrees with both doctors. They decide that she needs to be medicated in order to fulfill her role as a woman. Under their supervision, Julia swallows handfuls of primary-coloured pills each day. After years of good behaviour and successfully survived hospital galas and Rotary dinners, she realizes the zombification has been complete and she falls stiff onto the floor of her kitchen where her children step over her to get to the fridge for their after-school snacks. When dinner still has not appeared on the table, the children FaceTime their father to complain. Harris leaves the office at once fuming and picking up a bucket of chicken and some mayonnaise salads on the way home. They eat the chicken and goop with the plastic forks provided in front of the TV. Harris doesn't notice Julia's inert body on the ceramic tiles until he trips over her on his way through the kitchen. After the funeral, Julia looks at the lid of her coffin and feels very grateful for having had the shellacked acrylic nails put on by Ping the week before. She scratches through the lid and the earth and roams the graveyard with dirt filled nails in torn Lululemon for eternity getting her jollies once a year by terrorizing any children who dare to traverse the graveyard on Halloween.

OR

7 One afternoon while vacuuming up a deposit of Craisins between the couch cushions, Julia realizes that she too has wizened into a Craisin. She sets out to reclaim her verve by shopping at thrift stores for funky off brand clothes pairing together torn jeans and modified concert T-shirts with electric blue knee-high Doc Martens which she wears to clubs and dances on tables like only a MILF on the loose can, ultimately necking and fucking a recently released inmate and catching some terribly contagious sexual infection whereupon she dies in shame and abandonment.

OR

8 Julia trades the Honda Odyssey minivan in for a vintage Pierre Trudeau style Mercedes convertible, which she subsequently drives to California with Cuthbert. While on route they pass the Grand Canyon where, paw linked with palm, they Thelma and Louise themselves off the edge. Fortunately, Harvey Keitel is on hand to capture the incident on film.

THE
WILD
IN
YOU

THE WILD IN YOU

Away at university that first year, you received a dog for Christmas from a small-town, high school boyfriend who tried to hold on. It was a wild dog, husky cross. Eyes at times as blue as anti-freeze, at times as grey as stone.

Some people have eyes like that. He had eyes like that. They tremble and melt, a glacial lake you could dive in, then just as quick, they cloud and stare straight through you, looking for another drink, a place to stay, the next best thing.

Two months after the dog, you broke up with the boy. He said you broke his heart. You loved that dog. And that dog would run and run and run. That dog could never chase enough. You'd be playing fetch, then before you realized, he'd lose interest and be off in the opposite direction the ball slowly rolling in his wake. Once, on a cottage weekend, he jumped off a dock, swam across the lake and swiped a steak from someone's barbeque. Wild as he was, he always came home, if only to shred everything within snout's reach. You were forever apologizing for a chewed shoe, a coat, a book, a couch. Everyone said, can't keep a dog like that penned up in the city.

Then, a thoughtless roommate, an open door. You carried his body stiff in your arms, staring down at his blood-matted fur as you walked. Everyone said, dog like that wasn't meant to be domestic. Everyone said, dog like that was meant to roam.

You lie in bed too exhausted to cry. The red colon blinks, marks seconds of absence, pierces your heart with each flash. Then it becomes just two dots pulsing like blood through veins that connect you.

Is he standing at a bar downtown, full of students and drinkers and lonely bored people who don't want to go home, who don't have to go home, weaving stale stories, winning fresh ears, drinking up ego shots, lifting her hips to the bar? Thoughts of you long faded, you're just a days old shirt worn through at the elbows.

You tell yourself it doesn't matter.

It does matter.

Yellow Pages by the black kitchen wall phone. You drag your finger down the impossibly long and growing longer list of bars. Stupid. There are a million of them. Call anyway. Have you seen the baby's father? No one in here by that description. Liars all. You know the place is lousy with them.

Unlock the door. Lock the door. Unlock the door. Lock the door. You could wait. Could steel yourself for confrontation. The bassinette beside you whimpers. You pull her in, press yourself to her. You are all breast milk and fears.

The night you met, after endless martinis at the resto-bar he tended, he told you he overdoses on people at work. That he needs some way to cope. Trailed each sip with stories of better things he'd done with his time, more important things, exciting things. Solitary things that kept him so engaged he didn't have time to let his mind unspool. Tall ships, road bikes, tree planting. And while alone, said he'd ponder the achievements of nature over man. Was humbled by a hummingbird suspended in front of his face with wings that beat so fast they grew invisible. Man's not so hot, he said, over the clatter of ice inside a cocktail shaker, can't even make a hummingbird.

Together, on a futon mattress, on a bare wood floor, you lay. Said he's what David Adams Richards calls a true alcoholic, one who always has money to drink.

Bar fights, cut lips, sea storms, waves. Stories spun of kayaking from Lake Ontario, through the Hudson River, along the Eastern Seaboard and down into Key West, Florida. Almost swallowed whole by sharks, water, women along the way. Walked up to a restaurant in New York, he said, stole a lobster right out of a tank and cooked it over a fire. So many stories. Was it ever once the truth?

Door slams opens. Red numbers glow. A chair knocked to the ground? A second thud. Then quiet. He must have passed out in the kitchen. Soon the baby will wake.

This is not your life.

Stones lobbed at your second-story window as you slept. Like a vampire, like the husk of a person, he hovered, and you caved. You invited him in. Was it your bed? Or just any bed? You didn't care. You were waiting around for real life to start or maybe for that acceptance letter to grad school half a province away. Some nights, days too, the vodka would seep from his pores, and fill the room with its bite. You'd cradle his head in your lap and stroke his scruffy blonde mane. He'd struggle to knit sentences together about a father who hit him, a mother who fixed breakfasts of milky tea and Matinee Lights with the filters cut off. And he'd reproach his frayed self, say grief is self-induced, grief is not necessary. Rubbed raw by alcohol, he'd laugh, say, emotions are weakness, I'm becoming too human. Then you'd watch red numbers change, colon dots flashing, and in your skirt and sweater set you'd masquerade as a Kelly Girl while he slept the day away evaporating into life's ether by your return.

Salty skin. Wet matted hair. July nights across from the Mekong, air heavy with the smell of frying dumplings. Ice cubes between teeth trailed along hot skin. Your bodies fit together perfectly. He said you scare him shitless. Then he'd go missing for days, then rocks on the window in the middle of the night. Said he knew from the moment he saw you, you would be his, as though you never had a say in the matter.

And now you are.

He and the chef served you dinner at the bar, coconut curry, a glass of sweet fruity white. Disappeared into the kitchen while you ate, only to return with itchy noses. He asked if you wanted some. Okay you said, a bit. Your nose tingled, back of your throat numb. You were loquacious and witty, full of amusing anecdotes, you thought.

Another Sunday morning after, at the diner recuperating over brunch. Smoothed the napkin over the lap of your blue and white checked dress, late summer sun trickling in through windows and shining over the both of you, over your dark wood table, golden syrup over pancakes. You swung hands together as you walked toward the chef's apartment. Then tires squealed and a black Corvette peeled away from the curb. Angelo, the dealer, he said, steering your arm to the door. Inside, the chef sat red-faced and sweating on his black vinyl couch. He wiped beads of moisture that dripped from his nose with the back of his hand before they hit the mound of powder on the glass coffee table. He apologized for not being able to figure out how to open the windows of his new apartment.

You retreated to the rooftop deck. Glimpsed the parliament buildings with their spires of tarnished copper peeking through white clouds that billowed and floated across the sky. He pinned you up against the railing, smothered you with his mouth. Skateboard wheels on pavement echoed between brick buildings. He played with the hem of your dress. The glaze-eyed chef stared on from his plastic throne. You pushed him back a bit, told him you were moving away, going to school. He stopped pawing long enough to say, I'm not moving. Who said anything about you moving, you said.

Monday on your way to work, you looked out the bus window into sheets of rain. A plush Yogi bear lay in the street, green hat smeared with asphalt and tire residue. In the bus shelter a boy in a Leaf's jacket, with sandy blonde hair that will one day turn brown like everyone's, stroked the plastic barrel of a pistol. You walked out under the weeping sky.

September. Books and papers piled on your desk, lights dimmed, tea gone cold. Alone in a new city, struggling to comprehend what's to come. Then, stones rattled your window, arms warm and familiar.

And when the results of the test were positive, expectations were discussed, promises made and one small caveat.

I'm a character artist, he said, and feel no obligation to a society I don't understand.

Not a hummingbird, you said, a human being.

Six months after she was born, he did what he does to get you to say it. And then you do, and he is free. Matted fur and blood droplets on chrome are all that's left.

Some animals aren't meant to be caged.

This is your life.

So, you lie in bed next to her sleeping, breathing body, her eyes of sky and ice next to your own of earth and moss. And fear begins its rain, salt soaked and human, for imaginations that let us dream up stories that never will be so.

ALL
THINGS
IN
COMMON

All Things in Common

The summer her father left, the rope attached to Meredith's tire swing frayed and snapped mid-air, her legs still tucked inside the tire. When it hit the dirt and began to roll down the slope toward the water, she had sense enough to grab the trunk of a skinny poplar and hold on tight. At the oddest of times, she remembers hugging the tree with one arm and staring at the other, bent backwards from the elbow, lifeless, moving as if it existed independent of her body. On the way to the hospital, her mother cursed her father's shoddy handiwork, reliving an old argument about the safety of tire swings. Meredith knew she should've tested the swing before catapulting herself, thrill seeking, through the air. She hadn't used it since the previous summer and every cottager knows things deteriorate when neglected and left to winter. She wanted to defend her father. What could she say? She was eight years old and mute with pain.

Such childhood vignettes rush over her, as smooth and unyielding in their persistence as black night waves over pink speckled granite. Given the Friday traffic driving north this Thanksgiving weekend, Meredith knows she shouldn't give into memory, knows she shouldn't shut her eyes even if it helps her see more clearly, but she can't stop herself. There's something about remembered melodrama that brings out the kid in her. An angry honk from a charcoal Audi startles her back into her proper place, real life, or current life or whatever it is she is doing right now, that beyond obvious biological factors, probably couldn't be considered by anyone with half a heart as living.

Here it is October already, leaves have turned and fallen. It's as though she's been under the spell of a nefarious wizard, then opened her eyes, groggy, to the reality that she is about to turn thirty and has accomplished nothing. That she works at a Queen

West lingerie store catering to people and their unmentionables is nothing to boast about. How many years has she been trying to leave? To quit? To become the textile artist she's always imagined herself? It was the feel of the fabrics, after all, which led her to lingerie. Soft raw silks, shiny satins. Meredith will never tire of their touch. Caressing fabrics is how she spends most of her working days now. Walking too close to the clothes racks, encouraging slips to brush incidentally against her forearm, weaving velvet between her knuckles. That and daydreaming. And it's getting harder to muster up smiles for customers who are lip-locked in a perma-cool state of aloofness. Perhaps, she considers, as she changes lanes to avoid merging traffic congestion, a contemptuous smirk of her own might be worth perfecting. She sucks in her cheeks, raises her eyebrows, gives herself a condescending scowl in the rear-view mirror.

She drives past the hi-way hamburger Mecca they'd always stopped at when her dad was still around, before they could no longer afford extras. Farther along, gaping at both sides of the hi-way, Meredith begins to appreciate the commitment of trees, holding firm to their ground, full of purpose. She pictures herself standing there fixed on the shore of the lake, leaning in like one of Tom Thomson's proud jack pines, forever blown in one direction, deformed beyond her control, wind drying her eyes, straightening her hair. Except, she wouldn't be a proud jack pine. She'd be a big, pink splotch of flesh peeking out from behind an autumn birch, all obvious and waving and ruining the whole thing.

The leaves still clinging are resplendent—amber, mulberry, ochre, citron. Meredith's always favoured earth tones in her fabrics. Her latest triumph is a russet batik cloth inspired by the dying Virginia Creeper on the fence at the back of the Annex house she and roommates, Vanessa and Cheri, have rented for the past four years. She intends to transform the fabric into a skirt over the weekend. It's a strong cotton in shades of ochre, variegated by waxy crinkles, lines of oxblood and black creating a pattern that mimics the underbelly of an autumn leaf. Out of nowhere, a minivan revs and muscles past her. She wonders why the rush. Then again, Meredith has no one to meet.

What she most enjoys about the cottage drive is the snaky, gravel road along the home stretch. Only then does she feel far enough away. Her father had given nearly all the twists and turns names. Devil's elbow, the corkscrew, gravity hill. Though she and elder brother Jason had stopped using them a while ago, the names were always there in the back of her mind. Last year, just before the hi-way exit, she'd seen a white-tailed deer dead at the roadside, a bunch of people standing around looking more peeved than sad, not knowing quite what to do. Deer or not, Meredith gets the same feeling with all roadkill, raccoons, skunks, porcupines. She refuses to not be affected by the twisted splayed guts, by the rigor mortis paws grasping at air begging for one last chance at life.

As she pulls into the grass and gravel driveway, she shuts the car off and glides into park. Relief. Nights alone and fresh air have been rare of late. Meredith slings her knapsack over her arm, it nearly buckles under the weight, and begins the trek upward. The stairs are a patchwork of stone and cement, moss for grout. At the top, etched forever, is the year 1978 and the names Meredith and Jason underneath. It had been a hot summer that year and humid. And Dad's drinking had been particularly bad.

He and Uncle Herb spent their entire two weeks of holidays building stairs and drinking beer, Labatt's 50 stubbies. It was her job to fetch. What pride she had taken in being a helper, an accomplice in a sneaky plot to outwit her mother. Sometime during those two weeks, between swimming, fetching and tire swinging, Meredith's pale skin escaped protection, resulting in a scorching sunburn and monstrous row between her parents.

Where the hell were you? he yelled.

How dare you! she screamed. *If you hadn't been so busy drinking…* Their words dissolved into a fog of meanness that engulfed them in the humid air. Then, a deck of cards, or a cribbage board or an ashtray went sailing off the table or counter or dresser. Her parents spent twelve years playing an elaborate game of fifty-two pick-up for keeps. And, in the end, it was her mother who was left stunned, scrambling around to clean up the mess.

Meredith opens the pine door to the familiar smell of absence. Drops her bags on the brown and yellow braided rug, packs her groceries into the fridge, then dials her mother's number on the tan rotary phone before she can come up with a reason not to. It rings, rings, rings. Eleven times before she finally answers.

"Hi Mom, it's me. Did I get you away from something?"

"No, I just had to wash my hands before answering. I didn't want to get pumpkin guts all over the phone. Where are you?"

"At the cottage."

"The girls with you?"

Lying that Vanessa and Cheri had come with was the only way Meredith could think of to escape a full-blown family dinner with her mom's boyfriend Russell, his three teenage boys, and Jason with new wife, Marlene. She needed a weekend to herself once in a while, Thanksgiving or not, without a guilty price tag attached.

"What about Ryan? Did he get to come?"

"It's a girls' weekend. Besides he's doing his own thing."

"He's so nice."

She's always pulling for Ryan. And if nice means placable and dreamless then, yes, Ryan is nice. Does this make Meredith not nice?

"Well, I just wanted to let you know I got here safely and to say Happy Thanksgiving."

"Thank you. Happy Thanksgiving to you too, dear. And I hope you have a wonderful birthday. It's such a shame we won't be able to be with you to celebrate. I heard the weather is supposed to nice all weekend."

"Do you remember the day I was born?"

"Of course, I remember! It was Thanksgiving Monday and I had to eat hospital turkey."

"No, the weather. Rainy, cold, sunny?"

"I never thought about it. I was just glad you had all your fingers and toes. It's your father you should ask. He was out at the Fox and Firkin or Fricken Fox or what have you while I was in the hospital with my second episiotomy."

Her mother wishes her the happiest of birthdays one more time and Meredith manages to hang up. Divines a bottle of rye from the bottom of her bag, opens her legacy and pours a five-finger shot into a plastic tumbler. Beyond sewing and solitude,

Meredith has come to the cottage this weekend for two reasons: to remember and to forget. And what better place to think and drink than in front of the Headless Virgin. She clutches her tumbler in one hand, bottle of rye in the other, and heads down the path toward the lakeside shrine.

The previous cottage owners had either a strange sense of humour or been staunchly religious. Years after they'd gone, Meredith traipsed through the bush and discovered a crumbling masonry Mary, arms still spread wide in benediction. Erosion had done its best to decay, but you could tell that her robes, in their finer moments, had been blue. Superstitiously fascinated, all seven years of her, Meredith had taken the statue to her secret place by the lake to shield her soon-to-be confidante from a decapitating world. The Shrine of the Headless Virgin, as she had later christened it, became her refuge when the cards began to fly.

Today the Virgin is still shrouded from the more corroding forces of nature by a cavern made from craggy shoreline. As a child she sat cross-legged in front of the image and had never minded the damp. It's less reassuring now. She inches her shoulders in sideways, lies on her hip, feet poking out though the opening. As she grows increasingly intoxicated, the moldy chill and cobwebs become blessedly less off-putting.

Over the years, she's transplanted hearty wildflowers from the side of the snaky road to encircle the shrine, though the flowers today are only headless stalks. Better headless than heartless. She imagines the garden she might someday have full of useless daisies, asters, fleabanes, butter and eggs. Sheer wild frivolity, inspiration for her material designs. Though with gardens come houses and with houses come husbands and with husbands come children, and with husbands and children comes sorrow. The closest Meredith is going to get to marriage is spending time with Mr. Right For Now. And like her mother, she supposes Ryan is nice in every sense of the word. Nice looking, nice manners, nice family, nice job. Well, holding overhead microphones for television broadcasting at sporting events isn't exactly nice, but the money is all right and there are perks like interesting people to meet, travel expenses paid. It was good enough. Ryan was satisfied with good enough. But being too early contented with good enough can lead to mid-life breakdowns and Meredith has seen first-hand what happens to the woman when her man discovers that good enough isn't quite good enough. There's nothing like crippling responsibility to leave bags under a woman's eyes where her own ambitious dreams might once have been.

Meredith vows, Headless Virgin as her witness, to quit the shop the moment she gets back to the city. Time to unstick. Determined not to let this newfound commitment evaporate like a near empty glass of rye, she recalls the business name she's been drumming around inside her mind for years and begins to formulate a plan to transform her dreams into being. Tomorrow she will get up early, sew her skirt together and begin her new life as an entrepreneur. Sole Proprietor of Verry Cherry Inc. Fabric Designs. Each unique piece will have a trademark cherry hidden somewhere on it, a gimmick like Waldo. She's certain, has never been more certain, of success. She refills her glass just once more and imagines the red-orange of the harvest moon above the lake splashed across a silk shift dress.

Meredith awakens at noon, thirsty as hell, to her thirtieth birthday. Half the bottle of rye is gone and half the day as well. Sunlight screams in through windows and her temples throb with the promise she made last night. She marches to the sink and knowing she will likely regret it late tonight, pours the remaining alcohol down the drain, recoiling from the boozy stench as it swirls slowly to a trickling vanish. With shaking hands, she fumbles the skirt fabric as she prepares to work, chiding herself all the while for succumbing to the lure of the liquor, for sleeping the day away. She grips the material with her fingers and cuts through the sorrel-veined cloth. And desperate not to screw this up, leans her left elbow on the table to steady her hand so that she is better able to follow the chalk lines of her design, cutting against the bias of the fabric so the skirt will hang long and straight. The sturdy cotton, shorn of its excess, feels lighter, softer somehow, and she guides it with intention through the machine's piercing needle, pulling, and gathering the material like sheets of autumn leaves into folds along her arm.

Burning
A Illusion
Tonight

Burning All Illusion Tonight

Cary rocks back and forth over the cement edge of the plat-form in his black brogues. The partially enclosed arrival departure zone is lined with Greyhounds flatulating diesel exhaust up into the evening air of January. He blows into his hands while looking at his reflection in the terminal window wishing he'd done something before now about his beer belly. He'd last seen Shannon four years ago. She'd just started film school. He'd quit by then, working instead for his dad in the *real world*. He lights a cigarette. A toothless woman wearing a sleeping bag as though a ghost costume, head and arms poking through holes, drags a cart up to him and asks for a smoke. She toddles along gumming it then turns back motioning for a light. They smoke together in the din, watching their grey breaths purl and merge into the billowing bus exhaust.

Three Greyhounds nudge along, staggering themselves against the left platform reminding Cary of Canada geese in half V formation. The banner above the driver's head glows red, Detroit, and there's Shannon waving unselfconsciously from the window inside. Doors wheeze open. Black and brown-coated throngs emerge. A woman in red faux fur descends. Her hair is purple-black and cut in sharp angles. She tosses her head; Cary thinks he sees feathers fly.

She finds him, lunges, and shouts. Claps her arms around him. He tosses his cigarette. It rolls down the slanted platform hovering on the edge before falling into the street; his chin nes-tled in the crook of her neck, he watches it smolder. She strokes the hair above his ears. "It's so short," she says.

"I'm Briefcase Charlie now," he says. "Yours is purple."

"Deadly nightshade." She runs her fingers through, asks if he has any darts. Cary opens his pack jostling it to encourage a single cigarette to stand out a head above the others. Takes one for himself too. Cups his hands over hers so the wind won't kill the flame. She grabs his arm to still his gaze and looking straight at him says, "it's so good to see you." He hugs her, echoes the sentiment.

"Car's over there," he points down the street. Swings her pack over his right shoulder and walks through a film of snow on the sidewalk that leaves a trail of his and her footprints melting behind them into empty spaces, a train of lace. Two vagrants huddle together, backs against a building, their cardboard sign obscured by snow. Cary pulls a crumple of bills from his pocket and presses them into the man's mittened palm.

"Same old Cary," she says, squeezing him around the middle, feeling buttons and buckle and belly. "I can't believe it still runs," she says when they get to the car. "Didn't we take it to prom?"

"You remember," he says, "she's still running. All I need to do now is paint *My Nova Scotia Home* on the side and add a few flames." He throws her pack in the trunk. Flips the ignition over a few times till it holds.

Shannon examines her teeth in the rear view, smooths out lines around her eyes. "God," she says, "I look tired. And old."

"Nah, you look real good." He punches the radio dial with an extended fingertip again and again, cursing, grimacing, complaining about pop songs and DJ chatter.

"Prom seems like forever ago," says Shannon.

"I still have the picture," he says.

"You don't! I was a total disaster. Spilled salad dressing down the front of my one shouldered, big-bowed teal taffeta, slammed my dress in the car door. Rip up that abomination, please, for the love of all that is decent and holy."

Cary stuffs his hands into the pockets of his leather jacket, allows the car to idle, and gripes about the cold.

"It's always worse if you don't dress for it," says Shannon. "Why don't you try wearing a hat or gloves or something?"

"I'm not walking around wearing a blue Leafs' toque like a stunned twelve-year-old."

"You don't have to wear a child's hat from 1982."

"It's all the same. You think you look all cool in your black grunge rocker hat, then you see yourself in a window somewhere and there's Relic, like he jumped right out of *The Beachcombers*, starin' back. So how was Chicago anyway? The bus said Detroit, you called me collect from Windsor," says Cary.

"Last stop before Toronto. Thanks for accepting charges. I can always count on you."

"Of course. But if I had a girlfriend, it would have been a different story."

"I hate that," she says. Why can't you have a good friend who is a girl? If I had a boyfriend, I'd just tell him I was picking up my old friend Cary and ask him if he wanted to come meet him."

"It's different with girls," he says. "They get all jealous and everything."

"That's ridiculous," she says. "Anyway, what a trip. So, this guy gets on and sits beside me. We're talking and it's kind of interesting, he says he's a truck driver and a poet, so I ask what kind of poems. He says like for *Reader's Digest* then rummages around his black duffel bag. Pulls out a tattered copy showing me some cheesy rhyming love poems, not horrible, I mean, who am I to judge someone's poetry. Then he starts telling me about doing time and getting shot and how his ex-wife bit him. Rolls up his sleeve so I can see the bite mark scar. There was a big white-pink circle scar, like a lamprey eel bite or something, like a dentist model got all possessed and latched on. And then it got weird."

Cary laughs. "We should park at my place, so I don't have to worry about my car after having a few drinks. Were you with some guy in Chicago?"

Shannon nods. He asks what happened, why is she back. She doesn't answer right away. Taps her fingertips over her mouth and stares into the lights of oncoming traffic thinking they look like search lights. "It just didn't work out, she says. His wife got in the way. Or maybe it was me who got in the way."

"Oh Jesus."

"I know," she says, "I'm a horrible person. What about you? Weren't you with that Melanie girl who was like a teenager?"

"Oh. You heard about that. That's all over now. We were drinking too much. Kept getting on each other's nerves. I love this song," he says, turning up the radio.

Shannon asks what he means about getting on each other's nerves.

"She had this big cardboard box full of tapes," he says. "Every time I was watching something good, she'd dig around making all this crazy noise. And, you know the *Pulp Fiction* soundtrack? The very first thing that comes on is, 'I'm going kill every last one of you mother fuckers.' She'd blast that in the bathroom every morning while blow-drying her hair. Drove me nuts."

"So, you got dumped."

Cary laughs, "yeah."

"She sounds funny," Shannon says. "Bet I'd like her."

"You probably would," says Cary.

They walk to an Irish pub, Finn O' Something or Other, fiddle music throbs out onto the sidewalk luring them in. One of the smokers outside the double doors docs a jig, slips on his smooth soled cowboy boots, and falls flat on his back wheezing laughter. His pals all gather round. He fans his arms into an angel erasing the snow into cement wings. "After you," says Cary stepping over the angel and holding the door.

Shannon grabs Cary's arm insisting she get the drinks and he find a table. He refuses, says he's the one with a good job.

She persists says, you're always so generous, you picked me up, you're letting me stay at your place and everything, let me buy you a damn drink. He acquiesces, surveys the place, spies a table and inches sideways through the crowd looking back and pulling faces for her each time he squeezes past someone until he finds a tall table for two by the stage.

They clink glasses. Shannon asks, "So what exactly is it that you do?"

"I'm an insurance broker."

"With your dad?"

He nods. "Kind of. He's in a different department. I'm in sales." Cary uses finger quotes to illustrate: "I sell products to customers."

"Expensive pieces of paper and empty promises?"

"Ahhh, I knew you'd be like this. We all gotta go sometime Pete," he says. He throws a package of Belmont Milds on the table.

"I'm just poking," she says, fiddling with the cigarette pack. "You got a job and a place to live, that's awesome. Look at me— another victim of the rainbow."

"You'll find something." He reaches across the table to light her cigarette, watches her lean back in her chair, cross her long legs. "I'm going to get more drinks," he says, "it's getting busy, it'll save us climbing through the crowd later."

Shannon watches him, feels her tension uncoil. Cary, she thinks, is a pair of flannel pajamas on a cold night. She grinds her cigarette down into mush as Cary arrives with a round, cork lined tray full of drinks: tall glasses filled with peach liquid, pints of beer, short clear glasses with ice and bubbles and lime.

"I didn't know what you wanted," he says.

Back at his place, Cary offers Shannon a seat on the nubby beige sectional that swags in the middle like a hammock. The walls are nicotine stained white, the carpet, a dirty industrial oatmeal. He puts on Bob Marley's, "Burnin' and Lootin,'" and fills a blown glass bong with weed from a tin box. The coffee table is littered with back issues of *Rolling Stone,* guitar picks, a harmonica, an overfull ashtray. He fires up the bong, his suck-ing face glowing orange from the lighter, and passes it to Shannon.

"What happened to us?" Shannon asks. "We had all these big ideas. I really thought we could do it."

"Relax," says Cary. "You're only twenty-five. Most people have to screw around for a few years before they figure shit out."

"I don't know," she says. "I feel like my whole life has been one of those water wheel things: dipping in, scooping up all these almosts, and then, just when you think you got the world by the tail, it dumps it all out."

"Oh Shannie-poo, you're just bummed 'cause of that dickhead in Chicago. Fuck him. Look at me: Mr. Rock and Roll walking around with a brief case and a buzz-cut."

A glimmer of streetlight beams past the filigree barring the basement window and onto the rumpled Keith Richards and Tony Sanchez poster on the wall opposite. "Here," Cary says, "lemmie show you something that'll cheer you up." He retrieves a clear plastic ring box made to look like cut crystal from on top of the television. "Open it," he says. She does. It's a squashed Marlboro cigarette butt. "It's Ron Woods'. I saw him at the Elmo a few years ago. I was right by the stage, so I reached up and grabbed it and these security guards dove at me, but I held onto it."

"Somebody tried to stop you from taking a cigarette butt?"

"Hey! His lips, Ron Woods' lips have been on that, says Cary." He laughs out loud. "I know, he says, I'm crazy. I don't give a shit about clothes and fancy cars. I hate talking to people, not you, but people, like at work. No one ever wants to talk about making music or painting, or cool new comedy acts. All they ever want to talk about is hockey, or stuff they bought or some stupid show they watched. Who gives a shit! That's what's so awesome about hanging out with you."

Shannon nods, makes the bong burble.

"Look at this." Cary holds a snapshot of their group of friends from summer camp ten years earlier. It's on a dock in front of the lake. Behind the group of twenty counselors there is a brown hut filled with life jackets and canoe paddles, a big chalkboard sign. Shannon stares at the picture; she was fifteen. Back then she would have thought she'd be something by now. Have a job, a real relationship, a clue. Cary goes into the kitchen. When he doesn't return, Shannon follows still holding the picture. There is a placemat tacked over the kitchen window as a curtain. The floor is white linoleum with small black diamonds, the cupboards are few and made of melamine. Shannon laughs, uses a magnet shaped like a director's clapboard to affix the camp picture to the fridge. Cary pours her a glass of wine. "Let's watch *Goin' Down the Road*," he says.

"Did you have Professor Cardinal?"

"Yup. Canadian Cinema 101. All hail Don Shebib. So, we watching or what?"

"Okay," she says, "but I'm fading fast." They make it halfway through the film before Shannon says, "I gotta go to bed or you'll find me here tomorrow, lost in your soiled couch cushions with all the pennies and the lint nubs, all the seeds and stems."

"Sleep in my room," says Cary. "I'm going to finish watching, play guitar for a bit."

Cary's bedroom is damp and black like the inside of a beer can, and smells the same, thinks Shannon. A queen bed with a balled-up duvet dwarfs the room. Beside the bed is another ashtray and a Christmas cookie canister. She peeks inside. It's full of condoms. She laughs and flops onto the bed fully clothed. The pillows and bedding need a wash, but she's drunk and safe, comfortable, and swiftly passes into sleep.

When all the booze is gone and his last cigarette has smoldered into a finger of ash, Cary sets his guitar down and lies back on the couch. Tosses and turns awhile before getting up, standing in the doorway looking at Shannon who is sleeping face down on the right side of the bed. He sits back on the couch. Gets up, holds the frame of the doorjamb and stares. Advances to sitting beside her on the bed, stroking her hair then returning to the couch, poking through the ashtray for a butt, playing a riff, wishing he could make her stay.

He climbs into bed beside her, curls around her like a spoon. Rubs her neck then her back letting his hand drift ever slightly lower. He kisses the back of her head and then her shoulder.

Shannon feels him there, fastening himself around her and stiffens. She turns on her side away from him, muffles her face, her eyes, her sudden sadness with the pillow. Cary sighs and looks at the ceiling. Hugs her with his one arm tight, knowing that as soon as she can flee, she'll fly, and breathing in the scent of her hair and skin one last time.

FREE
A
R
O
T
E
L

Carousel

A cold gust came in off the lake causing the oaks and maples that lined the streets to lose their orange and red leaves well before they had a chance to turn brown and drop off at their own pace. There was something about fall that always made Chad feel sort of hollowed out. It wasn't just what had happened, what those boys had done to him. He'd always felt that way—that autumn was a bit of a ruse. It wasn't a long winding down into the gentle snow of a Christmas card, it was the sharp and sudden death of summer; the days darkened, the trees relinquished their leaves submitting to the disorder of the wind.

Outside, the sound of boots scuffling and laughter rose in the air as university students prepared to leave town boarding the late Thursday bus for home. Or, smug and settled into their fall programs, they were out drinking and making fools of themselves before Thanksgiving, the first long weekend of the school year. If things had been different Chad might have been with them, might have been one of them. He would know some of them, those who stayed, they had graduated high school around the same time as he was being released. He hadn't been well enough at the time to envy them, and he didn't see any point in envying them now.

The glow of the Mini Mart sign cast elongated shadows of streetlamps and tree trunks around the parking lot. They looked a bit like giant bars surrounding a cell, Chad thought, as he continued weaving layer upon layer of metal rings for his chainmail tunic. Had a surge of wind not brought in a heap of dry leaves through the glass doors along with a customer, he might have continued staring at them as he worked. He rose from the stool where he'd been weaving to grab the broom.

"Evenin'," the man said, whistling as he walked to the back of the store.

Chad watched him grab a drink from the back cooler, heard the faded murmur of Winwood's Valerie on the ceiling speakers, the squeak of his wet sneakers against the floor, the crinkle of a bag of chips grabbed on the way to the counter.

"Pack of DuMauriers, please."

He was older than Chad, but somehow younger too. As he turned to reach for the cigarettes on the top shelf, he saw the guy smirk and stood taller. It wasn't easy carrying around the heavy shirt knit of metal rings, but he was becoming stronger; the muscles in his legs made the thighs of his jeans taut and he'd grown accustomed to the burning ache across his shoulders. He stared into the man's face as he stuffed a plastic bag with dill pickle chips and cigarettes and root beer almost daring him to say something, daring him to test the fortitude of the knight. The worst had already come and gone. Chad no longer feared. Perhaps, he no longer cared. The man dropped coins and rumpled bills in Chad's palm from above so that their hands would not touch.

"Have a good night, eh?" he said, and then as he was safely on the threshold of the door, "Nice hood, dude."

Chad continued watching the leaves tumble along the asphalt before sitting down intwining the loops wondering if the girl with the gap between her front teeth, the one with the dyed black hair, skin white as paper, would soon be in for her scratch and win ticket.

★

Richard and Lydia argued in the living room so as not to interfere with Adam who was watching *Star Wars IV* in the family room. Richard was standing, gesturing grandly in the middle of the room, in the middle of a drawn-out tirade, no not a tirade, thought Lydia, more like a recitation, like a speech he'd rehearsed for who knew how long. She watched him as though watching a performance and thought he looked old. Not *old*, but now that he was shaving his head to compensate for his receding hairline, the imposed baldness pushed him into a higher age bracket. She considered shushing him or even interrupting, but was sure it would prolong matters, incite more ire and, really, what difference would it make? It wasn't as though Adam paid attention to their squabbles, especially not when Star Wars was on.

"You can't fix him," Richard said. "He is the way he is." And when Lydia didn't respond, "Who are you? I married an ambitious woman who couldn't wait to set up her practice one week and go wine tasting and cycling in Tuscany the next. Now," he waved his hands defeated, "now, you're giving up everything. If you want to be a martyr to the cause, go ahead, but not me. Don't get me wrong, I love the kid just as much as you."

Here, Lydia, had she been a foolish woman, would have begged to differ. Had she been a masochist, she would have given Richard several pointed, well-placed jabs to knock him from his horse of righteousness. She was not foolish nor was she a masochist. She allowed Richard to continue.

"But I can't save him and no matter how many doctors you drag him to, no matter how many nights you spend doing Google searches for autism cures, you're just going to have to learn to accept him the way he is."

Lydia had just taken a partial leave from her medical practice, had offered a spot to a young doctor who had recently graduated. It was the straw that broke their marriage. She explained that she needed more time for Adam. She had said when they discussed it previously, that if Richard spent more time at home with Adam and less time at the bank making sure his corporate clients were happy, she would have more time for her own work. She didn't bother to mention this now. She knew by his omission that he was culpable. And what Richard said was true: she had done much research and put Adam through many consultations. And now, as a result, Lydia had a plan of action. It was operation give Adam the best chance possible. Of the many naturopaths and nutritionists approached, Dr. Stavropoulos' recommendations for fresh green juice and whole, organic foods while eschewing gluten and dairy best fit the reading and research she'd done on the autism diet. He would monitor Adam's progress, but she would have to shop and prepare the food and juices, sneak in the supplements, take him for regular blood work and keep meticulous food diaries. How could she maintain such rigorous standards along with the responsibility of a full-time general practice? How would she take him to socialization therapy and speech therapy and… and… and? And when had sampling different Chiantis via bicycle in Italy suddenly become so much more important than the well-being of their son?

"Why can't we just enjoy our lives a little? That's all I'm asking. You can't control every facet of his life. You're going to wake up one day and he'll be out on his own."

"That's kind of the point Richard. Put in the hard work now so he'll be able to function on his own when he's older. He's five." What did he think? You dropped the kid off at school, picked him up at the end of grade twelve so you could shake his hand on the way to university? Lydia held one of the couch cushions on her lap and traced the olive and gold embroidery with her finger. She'd spent a fortune on those throw cushions. What on earth had possessed her? She started to say that perhaps her parents could come and stay with Adam sometime, but the words just spilled out of Richard. She would have to shout over top of him to make herself heard. He was saying something about that's the trouble with kids today: everyone who plays soccer gets a ribbon, kids never learn that sometimes you don't win. She thought such comments coming from a man of privilege who never lost anything in his life, a man who easily rose to the head of corporate accounts, were pretty rich. He wanted to enjoy the spoils of his life with an attractive, successful wife by his side without some fucked up little kid getting in the way, and then the universe said, Ha!

"So, some kids at school are gonna called him retard, he'll have to toughen up. That's the way kids are. And you know what? Let them. He'll be stronger for it, maybe he'll start to realize that you can't go around flapping your arms all the time if you don't want people to make fun of you."

"Richard," Lydia was incredulous, "Oh my God. Do you not remember what the very first doctor we saw said? Autistic kids aren't socially motivated. They're sometimes not even socially aware that's part of the reason I take him to therapy twice a week."

"You and your therapy. What does he do in therapy? Draw pictures? I'm paying through the nose so that my kid can learn to draw pictures of women in red burkas. What the hell is he learning from that?"

Lydia laughed though it came out as more of a scoff. He'd become ridiculous. "Those were Imperial Guards, from Star Wars."

"Star Wars. You think you're going to cure him by calling him Luke and making him drink wheat grass? You're not doing him any favours." He crossed his arms and hung his head dramatically on top of the white painted mantel between the large candlesticks. He paused for a moment, perhaps to give Lydia an opportunity to rush toward him in an effort to comfort, to counsel. "I can't do this anymore Lydia. I'm done." He grabbed the suit jacket that he'd hung over the railing when he'd come home, scooped his car keys from the table in the front hall, and left.

★

Muriel sat at the kitchen table with a piece of pink Bristol board, some scissors and glue, some pictures of herself and her son, and a whack of old magazines. It was a damp, windy autumn night, there was nothing good on TV and she'd been promising Crystal from work that she'd make a vision board for weeks. According to the book, *The Secret*, Crystal had given her, Muriel was supposed to create a collage of pictures that would help her to visualize the life she wanted. If she used her vision board to focus on images of her deepest desires, the universe would conspire and rearrange itself to help make these things manifest. So said the book, anyway. Crystal bought her a copy after Chad had been released and things turned out to be a lot harder than she'd expected. Muriel had pinned her hopes for so long on his being well enough to come home that when he finally did, his maladjustment was a surprise unraveling to them both. Physically, he was much better, still scarred most notably on his face, but better. Though he was worse in some ways too. He was no longer cheerful, and his boyish shyness had turned from endearment to impediment. How could any kid go through something like that and not be damaged in some emotionally lasting way? His happiness and well-being would be front and centre for her vision board. After all, she was supposed to represent all of her deepest desires, and imagine that they were already here, that she had already achieved everything she could ever wish for and then concentrate on how great she felt now that she had everything. That was what she understood to be *the big secret*: this Law of Attraction. If she felt good and focused on all the great things in her life the universe would give her more. Most of the time she believed in it, believed that forces in the universe, directed by the thoughts of individuals, swirled, and conspired around them. With Crystal it was religion. Crystal said that if it weren't for practicing the Law of Attraction, she would never have met her husband, the owner of a construction company who made more than enough to keep her in fake nails and hair extensions. Always they were jetting off to St. Lucia, or St. Kitts or Turks and Caicos or somewhere tropical and foreign sounding where Crystal could lounge in her bikini and have Gordon take pictures of her sucking in the sides of her face to emphasize the height of her cheek bones.

Maybe Muriel should put a picture of a gorgeous body on her vision board, and somewhere tropical as well. Of course, a woman Muriel's age didn't need to be flaunting herself in a two-piece. Although, she had always wanted a fit, toned body. She'd even settle for losing twenty pounds. Maybe she could cut a picture of someone else's body from a magazine and paste her own head on to it. That would be more authentic. Authentic maybe, but not realistic. Who's to say? Valerie Bertinelli was on the cover of *People* at 48 in a bikini, so why not Muriel? That was the thing about *The Secret*. The secret about *The Secret*. She could sit shoveling in Tim Horton's muffins every morning and never lift a finger at the gym and no matter how much she concentrated, or visualized her body changing, it wasn't going to change. She not only had to think and feel as though her life was as she wished it, but she needed to act the part of a fit person and a fit person would be eating celery and riding on a stationary bike. In moments of skepticism, Muriel would think back to something her ex-husband used to say: wishing and wanting is like sitting in a rocking chair, it's fun to do but you won't get anywhere.

She had a picture of Chad, a few pictures of Chad. She reached for his tenth-grade photo, marveled at his perfect skin and grey blue eyes. She knew this old school picture so well. She'd kept one on the fridge, and another on the mirror in the bathroom, and a third one on her station at work for years. It always surprised her how young he was. She had more recent pictures of him too, but her deepest desire was that he'd once again be the sweet innocent boy she'd known before the attack, and that was impossible. No Law of Attraction was going to change that. More recent pictures showed him with residual scars wriggling up the sides of his face like pink worms. And where his nostril had ripped and his nose shattered, there was an angry red line demarcating the upper left side of his face from the right. She'd given him a tube of coconut oil to smooth across his scars to help them fade, but his are not the kind of scars that skin grafts, gentle kneading, and special oils can fade with time and wishful thinking. No, she must put a current picture on the vision board because it was now that she wanted his happiness.

Muriel worried that something would happen to him working the Mini Mart until midnight. She approved of his working, of his getting out of the house and interacting with the public. But that crazy chainmail shirt. Tunic, he called it. He was always at it with that bucket of metal rings between his knees. It must weigh a ton. She couldn't get over the shirt. Nor could she bring herself to question his making of it. Was he creating some kind of armour to keep himself safe? It was of no consequence: it was not her job to judge; it was her job to love.

She didn't blame herself for what those boys had done to him, though she couldn't help thinking that if she'd had the courage to leave Tom earlier, Chad might have been more emotionally resilient. She was afraid of so many things in those days.

Afraid that if she left Tom she'd be poor, that she'd be warping her son by taking him away from his father, that people would talk. Tom proved his worth in the end alright, never once coming to visit Chad in the hospital, never once calling, never so much as a kiss my ass since they left him way back when Chad was in junior high. Anyway, that's what this whole "Secret" experiment was about as far as Muriel was concerned, it was time to stop beating herself up over things she couldn't change and to focus instead on her future, their future, and change those things she could. She cut out a picture of a beautiful beachside home and pasted it onto the Bristol board and then a horse, she'd always wanted a horse, then an airplane, a picture of New York in the spring and then, a picture of Chad. It was a current picture, but she took a red marker and drew a smile over his sullen mouth and on second thought, cut a pretty brunette out from a fashion magazine and glued her on beside him.

★

Adam knew that the end of the movie was coming. His mom sat on the couch beside him. That meant the movie would soon be over. He knew what the end looked like. It was black with white letters and music and if he kept watching it would stop and then the screen would go black. He would pretend that he made it go black by using 'the force'. Then it was snack and bath and teeth and book and bed. Snack and bath and teeth and book and bed. He pulled the Yoda action figure's cloak through his fingers. It felt soft and it made him feel quiet. He dragged the soft fabric along his lips. The black screen came on the TV, and he heard his mother's voice. He saw a picture of Luke's mother in his mind. Padme Amidala. Padme Amidala. White painted face. Great royal headdress hanging down like horns with gold dots.

"Ok Adam, it's time for your snack."

On a plate shaped like R2D2 there were green seedless grapes, a small dish of humus, a stack of crunchy rice crackers. Next to it sat a glass of thick green drink. It tasted sweet and like banana and would give Adam a green mustache. Yummy. Yummy. Yummy. He hummed to himself and clutched a green Yoda in his left hand with the cloak wedged firmly between his fingers.

"Anakin gone?"

"Yes. Dad's gone out for a bit."

Green juice, sweet juice, Adam repeated the words in his mind and rocked his body on the chair. Luke drinks green juice. Yoda drinks green juice. Padme drinks green juice. In his mind he watched the thick green liquid slide and twist down all their throats like the Grinch sliding around one of the Who's living room floors as he stole all their presents. Anakin gone. Anakin slammed the door.

*

It was getting close to quitting time, so Chad swept up the leaves that had accumulated into a pile at the door. When he realized the wind would just blow them back in, it was too late to stop. He regrouped, picked the leaves up one by one and watched his hands drop them in the garbage. Except for a few misshapen knuckles, his fingers were slender, the soft tips dotted with dried blood from all his wirework. They were strong hands, the hands of a grown man, though he seldom thought of himself in that way. Through the bars on the window, headlights shone. A man in a suit with his shirt unbuttoned at the neck and a red striped tie pulled loose from its knot rattled the handle, then he pulled instead of pushed. The man seemed agitated as he made his way around the store, eyes flashing between shelves; he paced the aisles as though he was looking for something the store could not provide and then, empty handed, approached the counter. Chad stared out at the man, his steel tunic heavy across his back. The man eyed him and his shirt with curiosity, with, perhaps, amusement, and asked for a package of cigarettes. He laid a bill on Chad's palm and fumbled around in his pants pocket for the remaining change. The corner of the man's mouth quivered, he seemed close to making a comment but in the end was unwilling to cause trouble for himself, or more to the point, commit to a connection of any kind. Chad stared down at him, he was tall he knew, and wearing the chainmail fortified him through distance. He tensed his jaw and turned his head so the man could see the thick cords of muscle flanking his neck.

★

When Richard returned home after his tantrum, he smelled of smoke. Lydia could smell it from where she sat on the wing backed chair with her feet up on the coffee table well into her second glass of red wine.

"Look," he said as he sat on the center couch cushion across from her. "I don't want to get into it with you again."

As though she'd been the one to start the something.

"I rented an apartment over by the university kitty corner from that old Mini Mart." She wanted to pounce on him for the smoking; she stopped herself from saying anything at all. He'd already rented an apartment. There was nothing now to gain. Or lose.

"Okay, Richard." Perfect timing, asshole, right before Thanksgiving. Truth was, she was relieved. Relieved for many reasons not the least of which was that she wouldn't have to spend all day cooking a feast that Adam would only turn his nose up at anyway, and one that would probably complicate Dr. Stavropoulos's meal plans. It was funny. All of a sudden, she had this odd surge of power in letting go of the idea of Richard as her husband. All those years she had argued back, had fought to make herself heard believing that her side of the story meant something when all along it never mattered—what good was a story told to someone who wasn't capable of listening? By not fighting back, by her refusal to engage in the conflict, Richard didn't know what to do with himself.

"I'll stop by on Saturday to see how you guys are doing."

"Sure. Do you need to get some things? The suitcases are still in the crawl space."

It didn't take long for him to fill a case and by the time he'd shut the door Lydia's wine glass was empty again and she felt nothing at all.

★

Friday morning as Muriel made her way into work, she saw that last night's wind had stripped the trees. Bunches of russet leaves cartwheeled along the roads and the sun shone brightly. It was a beautiful day. She reminded herself of *The Secret's* mantra: I'm so happy and grateful for this beautiful day. The key stuck in the lock. Muriel, with her enormous pink purse slung over one arm and juggling a paper bag with a muffin and an extra-large cup of coffee with the other, jiggled the key eventually turning it to open. It was a two-handed feat she attempted with one. She must have been a sight. Story of my life, she thought, as she pushed the door open and squeezed the paper cup too hard at the wrong spot causing the cup to dislodge from the brown plastic lid and spill warm, sticky coffee down her arm. She looked at the black leather drying chairs and considered slouching into one of them and having a good cry. It was too early for tears. Rein in the negativity she reprimanded and set her coffee on the reception counter wiping the spill with a paper towel. She practiced the Law of Attraction, of gratitude as she set about her days work. I am so happy and grateful for this moment, I am so happy and grateful for this day, I am so happy and grateful to be alive, I am so happy and grateful that my son is alive and well, that I have a good job I enjoy, that I am well. The forces at work in the universe only want the best for me. And for Chad she added, though she wasn't entirely sure she believed it, and wasn't sure he was that well either. I'm so happy and grateful for my life, I'm so happy and grateful to be alive, I'm so happy and grateful my son is alive and well. If she willed it, if she was persistent and genuine in her thoughts the universe would make it so.

Muriel took a sip and began flipping through the appointment book. Fridays and Saturdays were always the busiest time of the week, she'd be booked solid until eight tonight. A hard day, but she could take breaks and a few long days toward the end meant shorter ones earlier in the week, plus, it paid the bills. And now that Chad had a job of his own there might even be a little extra that she could save up, for, well, for a trip to St. Kitt's. If she believed it, she'd see it.

Lydia Payne, the doctor, was booked for 9:30. Imagine, a doctor with a name like Payne. That always made her giggle. Lydia like to have her roots touched up every six weeks and booked routinely for six months at a time. She had a busy life that woman, always working or taking that boy of hers to some kind of therapy. At least Muriel had had fourteen beautiful years with a perfectly healthy, normal child and when he got over this phase of dressing like a medieval knight from a video game, he'd probably make some more friends. It was just a phase he was going through like when he and his friends from junior high went around ripping the sleeves off their plaid shirts in the name of fashion. She thought of when Chad used to bring friends home for dinner or to watch TV. It seemed a lifetime ago. It would just be the two of them again this year for Thanksgiving as it had been since he got out of the hospital. Not spending another holiday in there, that was something to be grateful for, though the staff, the nurses especially, took very good care of them. She'd made a few new clients as well. There was always something to be grateful for.

Muriel switched on all the lights in the salon, turned on the ambient music channel, pulled some towels out of the dryer and began to fold when Crystal tottered in on her heels. She was pleased to hear that Muriel had at long last completed her vision board. Now just wait and see she said. The phone rang, the first client arrived, the day had begun.

The doctor hung up her coat and said hello. Muriel waved from the back thinking she always looked so beautiful.

"What can I do for you today, Lydia?" she asked as she draped the black nylon cape around her shoulders.

"Shave it all off and save me the trouble. Do you style wigs?"

"Bad hair day?" Muriel combed out the thick brown hair and ran her fingers through.

"Oh, not really. It's just, have you ever wanted to completely change everything about your life from what you look like to who you are? You ever feel like running and screaming away from who you've become?"

Muriel nodded. Lydia felt stupid and small. Of course, she had. What that poor woman must have gone through. She grabbed for the hand that combed. "I'm sorry. I know you have."

"Any special plans for Thanksgiving?"

"Nope. Nothing. It'll probably just be Adam and me."

"Richard out of town?"

"Yes."

"You decide on a colour?"

"Hot pink and I want a thick fringe."

Muriel laughed. "I could highlight with red, or put in some burgundy streaks?"

"Would that look good?"

"Why not? It'll be different, that's for sure?"

Different. Yes, different would be just great.

Muriel clapped her hands and left for the back room to mix the colour paste into the little black dishes. Lydia wondered if she should have mentioned that she and Richard were separating. Hairdressers and bartenders made the best listeners, right? The thing about no longer pretending that everything in her life was perfect was that she'd been doing it for so long. After all those years of playing pretend, once she stopped all that was left was the truth, and it sat staring back at her as empty and ugly as the middle-aged woman sitting across from her in the mirror.

Adam, 'Luke' as he asked to be called, was spending time with his speech therapist this morning. Usually, Lydia would stay and observe and sometimes participate. Melissa, the therapist had asked her not to, though she hadn't used those words, she had gently, repeatedly, suggested that Lydia probably had other important things to do or invited her to use Adam's therapy time to do something nice for herself, said she likely needed a break. Lydia didn't want to leave Adam there. Who would look out for him? She'd stayed a little longer than Melissa had wanted, but after watching them talk about Star Wars and play with the light sabers, that was part of Melissa's technique using what interested the child, she eventually did leave. And wondered, as Muriel painted her hair and bound the coated strands in foil, if some of the things Richard had said to her last night were true.

★

In history class that morning, after Chad had folded himself into the chair and tucked his long legs underneath the desk, his teacher asked if he intended to write the required essay on the feudal system. Chad nodded and looked down into the sea of silver rings in his bucket and said nothing, just continued inter-locking circles. The class giggled. No one bothered him about school much after what had happened. And any teacher worth his salt would understand that in his short life, Chad had already learned so much about power and injustice.

It had been nearly three years since he sat in a classroom like this. He heard them talking in the halls too, heard them they say that he was the one. For two and a half years he'd been in and out of hospitals and rehabilitation centres; adults told him things he needed to do like make up for lost time, catch up with the rest of his peer group, but he could not imagine going back—who would he be?

He'd still been a boy, a child when they came upon him cut-ting through the golf course that night. He'd begged his mother to let a friend drive him home from his first high school dance. He could not bear to have her waiting in the battered Chevette outside of the school's front doors. But there was no friend, only spindly-legged Chad in his tan pants, his arms too long for the sleeves of his white Oxford button down. His gross motor con-trol had not yet caught up to the growth spurt that had started and would continue throughout the next two years on his hos-pital bed. He wouldn't have known they were growing pains then, he'd just feel more of the same: the soreness of his stretch-ing body compounded by the mending of broken bones, the healing of skin and ligaments. All his mother, all the police, all the school personnel, the hospital staff, the newspapers could think to say was why. Why had this gang of boys done this to Chad? Chad knew the answer. It sat a sour puddle in his stomach and rose and slunk up to his mouth sometimes reminding him.

· *Why you wearin' such a gay shirt, faggot*, the one with the red cap jeered, ramming a baseball bat into his stomach. Then another voice, a heavy boot at his back. Chad said he was at the school dance, and they'd laughed and pushed. He had cowered when they circled and descended, as he'd seen his mother do to shield herself from his father's fist a hundred times before. All Chad had wanted was to dance with Leah Monroe. He'd been too scared to ask and had spent the evening instead making awkward conversation with a pimpled kid he barely knew, the two of them lingering in the shadows of the dimmed gymnasium all evening long. A black hoodie tripped him as he tried to get away, kicked his side, stomped his spine. Chad heard shouts, felt blows. Heard his father's voice in his head. The boys were pent up hounds ripping apart a long sought-after fox; he felt his teeth go, then the bat hit his head and he remembered nothing save for hospital beds and worried faces.

★

That night at work, Chad passed the girl with the gapped tooth two Scratch and Win tickets across the counter. She smiled. He tried not to. He watched her pick at the metallic square with a thumbnail coated in chipped, black polish. He passed her a penny from the give a penny get a penny need a penny take a penny dish. Woo hoo! I won twenty bucks, she squealed raising the hand with the penny in the air. Chad opened the till and gave her the cash. She bought several more tickets and handed one to Chad. Their fingers touched and they scratched their tickets together in the fluorescent tinged silence until the door swung open and a woman with a kid in a white karate suit holding a light saber entered. They walked toward the fridge at the back. Halfway there, the mother turned back and looked at Chad, squinting her eyes. The girl with the tickets said her name was Jenny, said that there was a concert coming up that she was going to with a bunch of really cool bands all the way in L.A. that her friends from church were hiring a coach to go on a kind of pilgrimage to this Christian rock festival called Paradise Found. She reached in the large, green canvas sack hanging over her shoulder and gave him a photocopied pamphlet.

"Obi, Obi, Obi!"

Adam danced around like a freak show, saying Obi, Obi. Lydia hated when he did that in public. He pointed at the blonde boy at the cash and said, "Obi. Obi."

She crouched down so that their faces were level and held his shoulders firmly in a futile attempt to look in eyes that could not focus. "Luke," she said. He turned toward her, at least. "Shirt! He's a, he's a, he's a knight." She looked up at the young man at the cash register noting a faint resemblance to the *Star Wars* character. What in the name of God was he wearing? He looked oddly familiar. Was that Muriel's boy?

"Yes," she said to Adam, "he has an unusual shirt. Let's get the cream for Mommy's coffee." They headed toward the cash. "You must be Chad?"

He stared at her, nodding slightly. She could see now that he did not welcome such questions, but it was too late, she was already in the middle of it and her tongue had already decided what to say and held the words in the space of her mouth regard-less of her mind's efforts to halt the proceedings. "Muriel's boy?"

"Obi, Obi."

Adam jumped toward the counter and knocked a row of Coffee Crisps to the floor. "Careful, Adam." Red faced, Lydia knelt to pick them up and restack them on the shelf apologizing as she worked. Would it ever get easier? She half knew the answer. One thing Richard had said resonated. She needed to start accepting Adam's abnormal behaviour as normal for him. This kid, Muriel's boy, he didn't care. He was wearing a shirt of metal rings. "Your mother does my hair. I saw her just this morning."

Chad still said nothing, put the cream in a bag.

"Shirt. Shirt, Obi."

"My son loves your shirt." Adam looked at Chad's face and Lydia thought she saw the trace of a smile on the elder boy. On the way to the car, Adam hummed and turned circles on the sidewalk. She opened the door and before hurrying him inside, squeezed him. He turned as she did so all she got was his back toward her front. That was fine with Lydia she still could smell his hair and nuzzle him. He didn't struggle against her he simply went stiff like one of the action figures he played with, firm and rigid like a like a Storm Trooper she thought.

"Come on, kiddo, strap yourself into this old pod racer and let's get back to Tatooine before the Jawas get us." Adam rocked in his booster seat, hitting his head on the back of the seat in front of him and slapping his hands on his thighs. There were still a couple of hours of daylight left and there seemed no point to the two of them to going home and sitting around. Though it was tempting for Lydia to consider putting one of the *Star Wars* films on continuous play while she wallowed in the bathtub, like any growing boy, Adam needed exercise. Perhaps they should get a dog. Kids on the spectrum are supposed to do well with animals. Temple Grandin said animals made her learn how to be human. Lydia would think about it. For now, they'd go on a hike together in the woods just outside of the city. It was exciting really, when she thought about it, now that she was only working part time, she'd be able to do these kinds of things with him. Simple things, things that mattered like hanging out with trees and rocks, enjoying some fresh air and exercise, and for dinner, smooth soup with no chunks—Adam style.

Adam carried the Yoda figure along with him on the hike enjoying the soft feel of the cloak between his index and middle fingers. These woods weren't like Tatooine, he thought, these woods smelled of pine and leaves and dirt. Tatooine was desert and had water farms. That meant it was dry and trees didn't grow there. Maybe this place was like Naboo where his Mommy came from. He ran in front of Lydia along the path rustling through the dead leaves, turning them up his wake.

★

"You want to go where?" asked Muriel. "LA? By yourself? With Jenny? Who's Jenny? This is the first I've heard about Jenny. How'd you meet her?" The words floated between them in the kitchen. It was Thanksgiving. This was the first interest Chad had shown in anything other than that shirt. Of course going to a concert with someone named Jenny would be a good thing for him. Why did it unsettle her so? She felt as though she'd been watching for signs of life and suddenly his eyes had popped open. Yes, she should do what she could to encourage any positive social behaviour. Still. She hated to think of him out there without her. But this was what she had envisioned for him all along. Getting what you want, thought Muriel, has a funny way of making you feel like you're in the middle of a *Twilight Zone* episode and you should have been more careful about what you wished for. She paused for a moment in her dinner preparations and mentally repeated I'm so happy and grateful for this day. I'm so happy and grateful for my life. I'm so happy and grateful my son is alive and well.

The turkey sat on the cutting board. Potatoes, green beans, and carrots covered and warming in the oven. Muriel stirred a saucepan of gravy on the stove, her hands on the long wooden spoon ringing round and round wanting, but not knowing what more to say, the smells of Thanksgiving all around them. Chad was in his armour at the table, his bucket of wire rings at his feet busy threading together metal circles without beginning, without end.

Acknowledgments

These stories were written, doodled, and picked away at over many years filling in the gaps and in between times of living and I am delighted and grateful that Chris Needham and the team at Now Or Never Publishing were able to help me share my vision. For early readings of select stories, advice, and mentorship, I would like to thank, Tracey Waddleton, Annamarie Beckel, Andy Jones, Joan Sullivan, Vaughan Dickson, and Graziano Galati. I also would like to thank my friends for their support and comradery: Niki Martin, Michelle Hodge-Brooks, Maureen Uren, Grace Egan, Janice Kinney, Jay Rothenburg, Jane Wallisser, and Janet Myers. Your trusted friendship over the many years we've known each other has been invaluable to me and I look forward to many good times ahead. A big thank you to my partner in life and crime, Doug Leeper, for all you do to give me space and lift me up. And, as always, thank you to my children for loving me and for keepin' it real. I am filled with love and gratitude. I am filled with loving awareness. Merrily, merrily, merrily, life is but a dream.